MURDER in the SNOWS

A. JAY

ISBN 978-1-64003-146-3 (Paperback)
ISBN 978-1-64468-539-6 (Hardcover)
ISBN 978-1-64003-147-0 (Digital)

Murder in the Snows is a fictional novel written totally from the authors imagination. If any part of it appears to be factual it is totally coincidental. The only actual facts written by the author are the locations in the Les Cheneaux area as well as Sault Ste. Marie and St. Ignace in Chippewa and Mackinaw County.

Covenant Books, Inc.
11661 Hwy 707
Murrells Inlet, SC 29576
www.covenantbooks.com

ACKNOWLEDGEMENT

I would like to thank and acknowledge the following: John Causley - Elder, Jeff Causley - Fire Keeper, Bob Causley, Stephanie Sabatain - Director of Native American Center at Lake Superior State University, all are members of the Chippewa Ojibwa Nation. Also to those who gave me information about the Dixie Highway being the old route to Cedarville and Hessel (M-134) before the lake shore route was opened. The Dixie Highway extended north to Rockview and east to M-129.

'I also would like to thank my professor at Lake Superior State University, Janice Repka, who is an author of many published books for children. Her efforts reflect in my ability to write.'

Two Shoes stopped for a moment, faced the fierce subzero wind that brought near frozen tears to his eyes and cheeks, and thought, There's more than one reason to pack up and leave for the day. It's getting dark, the fish haven't nibbled at the bait all afternoon, visibility is near to nil, and I'm getting cold. *He began packing up his fishing box.*

Suddenly, he felt a presence. As he turned, he looked up and saw a figure wearing a dark hooded jacket and holding a raised pipe-like object. The pipe slammed down on his head. Excruciating pain caused him to see red and then black, giving way near unconscious.

Struggling to keep alive, he saw red again as he felt another blow. Then his body was dragged, the back of his head banged on chunks of frozen ice. He felt ice-cold water shock his feet, legs, waist as he slipped into the fish trench. He grabbed the edge of the ice and felt his gloved hand freeze fast.

In a voice just above a whisper, he asked, "Why?" Then total blackness enveloped him as he sunk into the frigid water.

CHAPTER ONE

The Morning After

The sun shined brightly in spite of the exceedingly frigid air. Stubby arrived on the ice, coming from his cabin, which sat along the ridge to the west. He inched his way towards his fishing hole. Steam from his breath mingled with the cigar smoke as he breached the spans across the edge of the ice to the spot where he fished. He trudged his way through the snowdrifts using a seven-foot-long ice spud as a walking stick.

The day before, snow fell all afternoon and into the evening in Cedarville. An Alberta Clipper was followed with a fierce cold wind from the northwest, which drifted the snow in all directions. The morning sun glared across the ice of Les Cheneaux Channel, where the wind revealed bare ice. In other places, the snow was drifted two feet deep.

When he reached his fishing hole, Stubby chopped the ice that froze over since the day before. He skimmed out small pieces of ice using a handmade tool that had a cup-shaped netted wire. Stubby threw the small broken pieces of ice far from the trench-like fishing spot. It didn't take long to finish. He reached for his wooden fishing box that doubly served as a seat. After, he cleaned the snow off the wooden box that held his fishing pole and an old worn padded seat cover he sat with his back to the sun. He reached for his vest pocket to make sure the fresh minnows were still there.

Glancing across Les Cheneaux Channel toward an area that was shallower and without current, Stubby noticed that Two Shoes, his fishing buddy, had not yet arrived. He paced the twenty feet to chop open Two Shoes' fishing spot. He gripped the ice spud high and took aim at the hole below.

"My God!" he screamed with a shocked expression, taking two steps backward. Staggering, he fell backwards to the ice. His cigar flew from his mouth, rolling across the ice into a snowdrift, while the ice spud fell, spinning away to his right.

What he believed he saw was Two Shoes, his eyes staring from his frozen face. Some of his long frozen hair flowed outward on the ice. Below the ice, his remaining hair floated below in the water. Stubby fell to his knees and crawled over to make sure it was Two Shoes. He frantically brushed the fine layer of drifted snow away and looked closely, giving him no doubt. Two Shoes' right hand gripped the edge of the ice where it remained frozen.

Stubby jumped up and frantically ran two hundred yards off the water to the office of Smith's Landing. Panting and short of breath, he reached old man Smith's back door. With closed fists, Stubby pounded loudly, yelling, "Smith! Smith!"

Smith yanked the door open. "Hey, Stubby, the door's unlocked. What's all the ruckus?"

"I need to call Sheriff George right away!"

"What's wrong? What's going on?" Smith asked.

"I just found Two Shoes, he's dead."

"What? Good God, how did that happen?"

"I don't know."

Smith pointed to the hallway where the phone hung on the wall. Stubby lifted the receiver and cranked swiftly to get the operator. "Hurry, hurry connect me with Sheriff George. I have an emergency."

"Right away, Stubby," the operator quickly responded.

Stubby heard it ring. "George, I need you over here right now! I hate to tell you this, but I just found Two Shoes looking straight up at me through the ice in his fishing hole!"

"What? Who is this?"

"It's me, Stubby."

"You're saying Two Shoes is dead? I'll come right away. How did this happen, Stubby?"

"He was in the ice in his fishing trench, staring up at me, when I looked down to chop the fishing spot open for him a few minutes ago."

"Where are you now?"

"I'm with Smith at the main office."

His gut wrenched. "I'll be right there."

George quickly grabbed his Kodak camera and an extra box of film. Maria Sutherland, the news editor from across the hall, questioned him with her eyes.

George poked his head in her door, looked at her, and said, "I have to go, there's an emergency."

"What has happened?"

"Later, we'll talk later."

George was grateful to Maria for giving him her father's office space at the east end of the newspaper building ten years prior after her father passed away. She had been a loyal friend. He waved to her as he walked out the front door.

He headed his new 1947 Ford pickup west on M-134 and then after one mile, he turned south toward Les Cheneaux Channel. His heart beat rapidly. Two Shoes was his best friend in the world. They were blood brothers since the second grade when they cut small slashes on each wrist and held them together in a special ritual that only second graders could.

As he drove, he thought how he had known Two Shoes ever since the first day of school at the age of five; at that time, they were lost in a new world. Their whole lifetime rolled past his eyes. Throughout their entire lives, they hunted, fished, and in later years had many good talks over a beer or two at Cedarville Bar. *I can't visualize Two Shoes dead in the water*, George continued to think. Two Shoes was an avid fisher, hunter, and now after the war, he lived a low-key lifestyle. He trapped and was very proficient in each task. How did this happen? Did he slip or lose his balance?

George turned in to Smith's Landing. He noticed that no one was stirring in the camp area, only a few cars were parked near a cabin where each separately speckled the waters' edge. No lights were shining in the cabin windows. Smoke trickled out of the bait shop, so someone had been there this morning.

The sun slid under a cloud, leaving a gray color to the snow and ice. The wind had pushed on to a quiet still. George pulled up the short horseshoe drive at Smith's Landing where he watched Stubby step off the porch to meet him. His long legs quickly reached George. Stubby pointed in the direction of the spot where he discovered Two Shoes. "I hated to be the one to tell you this. I know how you felt about Two Shoes."

Side by side, the two quickly approached the ice, silent in thought. George looked at the tracks Stubby made earlier, hesitating to reach the spot where Two Shoes was. He looked around for any other tracks or clues, he knew without recourse that he must look at his buddy. He took a couple camera shots at the tracks and snow drifts that approached the death scene.

George was obligated to fight his inward feelings and put duty first. When he reached the frozen ice hole, he saw the ice spud sprawled to one side and a half-smoked cigar in the other direction. He clicked two more pictures. Then George looked down at the thin ice covering Two Shoes' head, narrow shoulders, and partial torso. His long black hair flowed outward, and his eyes looked peaceful yet empty of expression. He noted Two Shoes' frozen right hand gripped to the ice edge. *Keep yourself together, George*, he thought. *Your personal feelings must be reserved. Right now, you're the sheriff.*

George noticed a trace of blood at the ice edge and scooped a sample into a vial for the Mackinac county sheriff. He placed it into his jacket pocket. He took a close-up shot of the blood and then of Two Shoes. *He must have hit his head as he slipped into the water,* George thought. *How did this happen? Accidentally slipped? The blood appeared to come from the back of his head, so he must have grabbed the edge as he went in. But became unconscious almost immediately?* George mentally guessed.

"I'll break him loose, Stubby. You can help by getting Smith. I'm sure we will need an extra help to pull Two Shoes out on the ice. Bring a thick blanket so he won't freeze to the ice."

George hacked away at the edge of the hole, starting carefully to disengage the body from the mass of ice. Smith and Stubby returned before George was finished. Their breath steamed out of their mouths. Smith brought another ice spud to pry up a section to secure the whole ice chunk and avoid losing Two Shoes to the channel under the ice. All three wore somber expressions as they began the chore. Smith brought one corner up enough for George to hold on as Stubby chopped the final edge of ice that framed the body, releasing Two Shoes' slightly built body from the fishing spot. George had chopped a square big enough to allow the men to carefully pull the body out. The men grunted as the full weight of the wet clothes and ice frame came with a splash. Water ran off the heavy trousers and jacket.

They laid him gently on the ice and then rolled him on a woolen blanket to avoid freezing.

"Stubby, will you stay here while I call the medical examiner and the county sheriff? Smith, I'll need your phone."

Smith nodded an affirmation and remained alongside the body.

"How do you think this happened?" Stubby asked George as he turned to walk away.

"At first, all appearances seem to be an accident. He could have been drunk, slipped, and hit his head. I'm going to have to ask you two not to talk about this to anyone for now until I investigate it. Do you understand?"

Smith nodded his head, acknowledging the deputy sheriff's order.

Stubby raised his eyebrows and shrugged his shoulders. "Yes, I do."

George turned and ambled through the drifts and across the short distance up the hill, past Smith's rental cabins, along the driveway, to the main office.

As he entered by the side door, George headed towards the phone in the hall on the right. He reached into his pocket and pulled a phone number out of his wallet. He cranked the telephone for the operator.

"Hi, Stella, can you ring up this number? It's nine-five-zero in St. Ignace."

"That's the coroner's office, George. What's going on?"

"Stella, you know I can't say."

"Okay, I know. I'll get it right away," Stella said as she connected the sheriff's number. George could hear the snap as she chewed her gum.

Within minutes behind George, Smith came in and filled the aluminum twelve-cup coffeepot with water and filled the top compartment with coffee grounds. He placed the pot to brew on his woodstove. Then he added logs to fire up the red coals. Smoke rolled from the stove front as Smith slammed it shut. He waited in a chair beside the woodstove while George finished his call to the medical examiner and the county sheriff.

"Drake's Funeral Parlor, Henry Drake speaking," came the voice on the other end of the line.

"Hello Drake, this is George Kaufman calling from Smith's Landing in Cedarville. I have a dead body on the ice at Les Cheneaux Channel near Smith's Landing. I'll need you to come out to take the body in for examination and autopsy."

"Car accident?"

"Not that he was in the water frozen in the ice. I suspect he slipped and fell into his own fishing trough. He could have been drunk or lost his balance. It appears he hit his head and became unconscious. That would be the only reason he wouldn't fight to get out of that frigid cold water. I need you to make an official statement for the record."

"I'm putting my coat on as we speak."

"Thanks, Drake."

George finished and rang for the operator again. This time, she just said, "I know you need the county sheriff's office."

"Do you need me out there?" asked Sheriff Brown. "Or can you handle it?"

"So far I'm fine, I'll report to you as the investigation goes," George answered. "Drake will bring in the body, and then the pathologist will be called from Williamston, Michigan, to examine the body for a precise analogy of this incident. That's when you may want to go over the facts with me. Until then, I will continue to investigate on this end."

"Okay, George. If you need me, just call. I'll document this in the log."

George hung up, heaved a sigh, and looked at Smith.

Smith had filled a thermos of coffee for Stubby. "I can take this to Stubby," George said. "Do you suppose you can bring Drake down when he gets here?"

"Sure, George, I'll help you in any way I can."

The coffee was almost gone when Drake arrived just over an hour later. Drake stopped in front of Smith's Landing and waited in the medical examiners' wagon, which he doubly used as a hearse.

Smith went out to greet Drake. "Hello, Drake, George is down on the ice." Smith shook his head. "This's some nasty business…Two Shoes being his best friend and all, I'll take you down. You can reach him closer if you use the circle drive, I'll show you."

George signaled to Drake and pointed across where he could get closer to the ice.

Drake drove the wagon into a larger horseshoe drive, which passed the cabins where he came nearer to the edge of the ice.

Drake went to the back of his wagon and pulled out a stretcher. George met Drake to help him carry the stretcher.

"Wasn't Two Shoes your hunting friend?" asked Drake.

Drake looked at George, who silently nodded his head.

"I'm really sorry, George."

"I'll miss him, for sure." His voice broke. "Thanks."

Stubby was sitting on his fishing box, puffing on the cigar that he'd rescued from the ice. He remained silent and didn't offer conversation. He had covered Two Shoes with an extra wool blanket from his fish box. Drake and George slipped Two Shoes into the body bag and zipped it up. Stubby helped the two set the body gently on the stretcher. Drake and George carried the body in an even cadence to the back of the coroner's wagon, where they stopped once again before Drake unlocked the back doors.

Stubby followed as they carried Two Shoes and helped lift the stretcher into the wagon. As they closed the back door, Drake paused and turned to look at George who stood silently with a gaze that looked off across the channel where it met the horizon.

Drake looked at George and began a narration that seemed to come routinely, almost as though he was thinking out loud.

"Funny thing about finding a dead body in the water. This one, your friend, Two Shoes, was floating. Normally, this tells me that he sunk for a couple days and then rose again. In this case, it appears that he knew he was going into the hole in the ice and grabbed the edge to try to stop himself because his gloved hand was frozen to the ice."

George let out his breath. "I noticed this too and took some pictures of it. I need to begin an investigation as soon as possible. Right now, my mind is filled with multiple questions, and I'm trying to decide where to begin to find answers. I hadn't seen him for a few days because he has been busy with the traplines. I wanted to talk to him on Thursday but didn't see him. He was probably up on his northern trapline."

Drake interjected, "Okay, so he could have been here longer? Why I'm saying this is, if he sank, it meant he drowned, but obviously he didn't sink because of his hand. Our examination will tell if there is water in his lungs."

"I figure he slipped, lost his balance, and fell into the fishing hole," George said.

"If he slipped and fell, he would have struggled and have taken in water. Did you notice any sign of a struggle in or out of the water?"

"No. Unfortunately, it snowed all day Friday and drifted during the night. That would have covered any clues," George said. "I believe he was stunned by the fall and conscious enough to grab himself before he went under. Probably he become unconscious right after. Because of the frigid temperature, the wet gloved hand froze instantly to the ice.

Drake weighed his words. "This is what I will have to relate to the pathologist when he arrives from Williamston. I'll call him when I return. He will need at least six hours to drive the distance, depending on the weather and road conditions down there and the wait for the ferry at Mackinac City. He may not arrive before late this evening." Drake went back into his narration, almost to himself rather than to anyone listening. "How long he was in the water is the question. Did he come here yesterday morning directly from home to fish? Unless he went for lunch at the bar, had a couple drinks and a sandwich, then returned intoxicated, slipped, lost his balance, and hit his head as he slid into the water. I don't know. That's something we'll have to find out." Drake reached for the handle to the door to the cab.

"I don't know either, but I will say I have never seen Two Shoes totally that drunk. I'll be waiting to hear as soon as you have the examination and report completed," George continued. "I don't know what the weather was in St. Ignace yesterday, but here, it snowed late yesterday afternoon, and it kept snowing all night while a westerly wind came up during the earlier hours of the morning. But let's suppose that he did lose his balance, hit his head, and slipped into his ice fishing hole. What caused him to lose his balance and slip into the ice? Two Shoes was an experienced ice fisher. He knew the dangers of falling into the water, even if it isn't deep on this channel."

Drake raised his hands and shrugged his shoulders. "And why was the body at the surface? Only one occasion in my career. The remains did not decompose because of the temperature of the water and remained floating because the ice froze before he could sink." He added, "The temps did fall with the wind from the northwesterly overnight."

"Here is a sample of the blood I collected from the edge of the ice for you." George handed the vial to Drake. "An investigation will give me more to go on, for instance, if he was seen, when, where, and by whom, something for me to go on. I'll fit it all together as soon as I have more answers. Like I mentioned earlier, Two Shoes usually didn't get drunk, just relaxed."

"George, even though we can test this blood, we don't know enough about it for accurate results. Zimmerman from Williamston will give the final report. Considering this, I won't have an answer for you before the first of the week."

Drake placed himself in his seat, turned to George, and said, "I'll call the morning after Zimmerman leaves." Then with a grunt, he drove off.

George grinned to himself and thought, *I need to lose weight.*

Stubby mumbled something about not feeling like fishing and turned away from George in the direction of his home.

George glanced in the direction where Stubby fished to see that he had put his seat and fishing pole away.

"Stubby, did you and Two Shoes fish together on Wednesday, Thursday, or Friday?"

Stubby stopped and turned towards George. "Wednesday, that was the last time I saw him." He turned and continued on his way.

George knew his next step would be to go out to tell Two Shoes' parents their son was dead. He nodded at Smith and stepped into his pickup.

Letting out a deep sigh, he backed the pickup out of Smith's drive and headed towards Cedarville.

George had only driven a short distance when the weight of the morning had caught up to him. He pulled his truck to the edge of the road and opened his mouth wide to release his anguish, but nothing came out. Instead, his throat constricted, almost shutting his breath off. He gasped deep breaths and then exhaled slowly. Finally, the sobs began.

The ache in his heart overwhelmed him. He sat for a while, calmed down, and was ready to face Two Shoes' folks.

CHAPTER TWO

Breaking the News

Seeing Two Shoes' parents would have to wait until he had made a report of the events that led up to this hour. He would need to go to the office to make it out while it was fresh in his mind.

Luckily, the lights were off in Maria's newspaper office. He looked at his watch and noticed it was noon, so she may have gone home for lunch.

He sat quietly at his desk. He could look across the hall into the news office through the windows that were above the half-wood paneled walls that divided the two offices. Probably old man Sutherland liked to look over at the paperworks from that vantage point and know what was happening without having to leave his chair.

George pulled out his record book and began the report. He looked at prior events. The last entry was only a couple days ago. Before that, there were sporadically dated trivial entries. Joe Spiro was arrested for wife beating again, which seemed to be routine every time he got drunk. Old lady La Plant lost her cat and needed George to help find it, and before that, there was a bloody accident when a fisherman cut his hand cleaning his catch. It was serious enough that he was taken to the hospital in Sault Ste. Marie. The most recent entry was the robbery at Principal Peabody's home just this week. Approximately three days prior.

Reaching for the ink pen and ink, he began. By far, it was the most difficult in his twelve years as a sheriff. His best friend was dead.

He had to routinely write everything down as the events unfolded. He wrote a full description as he saw it take place. Each time he began, he hesitated. Finally, he took a deep breath and worked his way through each event. As he proceeded, he came up with more unanswered questions and reached for a tablet to write them down. The list would be addressed later today if time allowed.

Content with details, he pondered for a moment to think back and reread the report to make sure he had not left anything out. Satisfied with what he read, he closed the journal.

He looked at the Ingraham pendulum clock, which struck one o'clock. It was time to go out to see Two Shoes' parents, Chief and Rowena.

Once in his truck, he headed north on M-129 to the first road east. He turned right at the second drive. As he drove down the two-track path to the log cabin that snuggled in a grove of pine trees and cedar where the sun streaked through here and there, shining through the snowy air, George caught the sight of a white owl descend and perch itself on Chief's mailbox. Its head turned and looked at George. Smoke from the woodstove curled into the sky; old wolf dog came to greet him. Silently wagging his tail, he accompanied George to the cabin door.

Before George could knock, Two Shoes' father answered the door. George took off his hat and held it in his hands.

"I…have some news for you and for your wife."

Chief motioned George inside.

"Rowena, come join us," Chief called to his wife. "George is here."

Rowena pulled aside an aqua color curtain that covered her bedroom entrance and came into the front room to join the men. Her forehead was furrowed with a look of concern. She wore a long house dress with a bibbed apron covering almost everything. Her thick long salt-and-pepper-colored hair was in a braid that hung down the middle of her back, which was customarily this way while home.

"Please do sit down." She gestured towards a chair. George looked around the knotty pine paneled room that held so many memories and the same furniture: a couch covered with a red flowered throw, lace curtains at the windows, one lamp, two chairs and a couch, and a Motorola radio sitting on a bookshelf in the corner. Old paint flecked metal folding trays were used for end tables. The wooden floors were covered with handmade throw rugs that Rowena had woven.

Rowena sat next to Chief on the couch. The couple looked straight into George's eyes, wondering what news brought George to their home. Rowena held her hands in front of her apron.

George stood and began by saying, "This is a part of my job that is most difficult. I have been a sheriff for just over twelve years, and I find today to be the worst for me. I really don't know how to start."

"Sit down, George." Chief gestured to a chair next to the couch.

"Tell us, George, what is it?" Rowena asked.

"Early this morning, Stubby found Two Shoes. He was drowned."

A stifled cry came from Rowena. The two held each other close. Rowena buried her face into Chief's chest and silently cried. He reached into his pocket for his kerchief and wiped her tears away, kissed her forehead, and quietly comforted her.

After a moment of silence, Chief took in a deep breath. He looked out the window at the snow-laden trees and watched the wind gust overhead swirling the snow. He rocked his wife comfortingly.

"I wondered...when he didn't return last evening." He paused and turned away, looked out the window again, and remained silent for a long time. He looked at George in deep thought.

After a minute, Chief spoke slowly, gently. "In all the days you were friends, did my son ever tell you why most everyone called him Two Shoes?"

"No, he didn't," George answered.

"From birth, he wore the moccasins his mother made him until he went to school. Then we bought him shoes. He was so pleased. Looking down at them, he said, 'Two shoes.' We called him that ever since."

"I didn't know that."

"My Native name for him was **Pungusha Mukwa**, Little Bear. For his stature, he could hunt and run faster than most." He hesitated and then looked at George. "I thought he might have stayed in town with you last night."

"No, Chief, I haven't seen him for a few days. I wanted to see him, but he didn't come to town," George replied.

"He went on his northern trap run Wednesday morning. He said not to worry if he didn't return until Thursday, he would stay at his cabin. He stays sometimes, but I guess you know that." Chief repeated, "I thought he stayed with you last night when he didn't come home."

George was at a loss for words. He reached for Chief and shook his hand. Rowena was looking down at her feet.

Chief continued again quietly as though he thought no one was there. "I saw the white owl, it came and sat on the fence one morning looking at the cabin. That was a warning. The next morning, the white owl sat on the shed roof out there, you can see it from the front window. It sat there and looked at the cabin again."

George looked out the window.

"Then the next morning, the white owl was sitting on the flower box in front of the window sill, looking directly into the cabin. I suspected then there was something going to happen. I wasn't concerned until I heard it hoot. That is an unlucky omen."

George knew that in most Native American tribes, white owls are a symbol of death.

Chief gazed into space quietly.

George cleared his throat and asked, "What can I do to help you?"

Chief hesitated and then slowly and softly said, "I will gather the cedar for the purification bath and then call the fire keeper and the pipe carrier."

George accepted this as a dismissal. He reached for the door, turned, and said, "I'll let you know what the coroner says and how soon you can wash the body with cedar in preparation for burial."

"Thank you, George, I know how close you, two, were. *Gii waabamin niich kiiwe* until we see you." His wife nodded and added,

"*Bamapii*." George stepped off the small porch onto the gravel snow-covered path to his truck. He turned his pickup around and looked back to see the two stalwart silhouettes on the porch watching him as he drove out the narrow drive.

In the distance, George glanced at the mailbox. The owl was gone. He stopped at the road, looked up in the sky where he saw the owl flying high away in a northeast direction. George turned west down the gravel road towards town.

CHAPTER THREE

George Finds a Partner

George intended to go home, but after he checked his pocket watch, he noticed it wasn't time for his wife, Isabel, to be home from her job at the school, where she cleaned and maintained the building. He headed to his office for a while to add to the day's report in his journal. He documented his afternoon visit to Two Shoes' parents.

Maria stood in the doorway of the newspaper office across the hall.

"Good afternoon, Maria."

She looked his way and asked, "How did it go, George?"

"As good as it possibly could, Maria."

"I talked to Stubby," Maria said. "He didn't tell me much, but I hope you'll give me something."

"Damn that Stubby." He scowled. "We had to pull Two Shoes out of the water through the ice. That's all I know, and it's enough for your obituary notice in the paper."

"Oh, I'm so sorry, I know how much he meant to you."

She reached to comfort him but checked her movement. He couldn't look in her eyes; his grief was too heavy.

"We'll know more after Drake calls to report what Zimmerman, the pathologist from Williamston, finds in his autopsy statement. Thank you for asking. It seems good to have a neighbor close by," George added. He smiled and returned to his office.

After completing the notes about his visit to Two Shoes' parents to report, George left to go home, but for some reason, he turned into the Cedarville Bar parking lot. He noticed Robert Lightfoot's car, an elder with the Bear Clan, which gave him another reason to go in. He needed to talk to him. Stepping into the bar, he was temporarily blinded by the dimly lit atmosphere. His eyes had to adjust from the brightness of the snow.

Shortly, George saw Lightfoot and was not surprised to see him sitting alone at a small round table against the wall. It was expected of him to make space between the white man and himself. Lightfoot was a man who said very little.

On the other side, at the bar, sat a half dozen local men. One unfamiliar woman was talking to Bonnie Palmer, the bartender. Bonnie nodded at George, filled a big mug from the beer tap, and took it to George where he had joined Lightfoot.

"Can I bring you some hot stew on this cold winter day?" Bonnie asked George.

"No thanks, Isabel will have dinner ready when I get there."

"Just thought I'd ask." Bonnie smiled over her shoulder and returned to the bar.

George looked deeply into Lightfoot's eyes and got right to the subject. "I have some news to tell you. It's about Two Shoes. I found him dead this morning."

Lightfoot responded, "I was told about this earlier. It is sad for you, his parents, and those who knew him." Lightfoot talked in his soft low voice. "He will be missed by many. As you knew, he was my cousin."

"Yes, you as well as many others," George answered. The two sat and remembered how proud they were of him when he returned from the war. How he was honored at the pow wow just last fall. They remembered how changed he was. He was quiet, kept to himself, trapped, fished, and took care of his parents. Occasionally, he would go to the Cedarville Bar and have a couple beers, sometimes with George, but nothing was ever planned that way; it usually was coincidental.

"Because he was my best friend and because he was Native American, I wish for you to help me with the investigation, Lightfoot." George bluntly came right out with it.

"I was waiting for you to ask," he answered, sadly smiling.

"Keep in touch." George finished his beer and left.

Lightfoot nodded and slightly smiled as George left.

CHAPTER FOUR

The Robbery

As George walked towards home, he reflected on the two events that happened in the past week. Earlier that week, as he arrived home, he heard the telephone ring. When he answered it, Peabody, the school principal, was very upset and anxious because he had been robbed. He remembered that in spite of the fact that Isabel had dinner ready, he had walked across and over on the main highway to Peabody's home with his fingerprint kit and Kodak camera to investigate. He talked to Peabody and asked questions. Peabody was upset and asked George not to tell his wife the exact amount of money that was robbed from his safe.

He remembered how Wendell Peabody told him that his wife, Tilda, was playing cards with the ladies, and he was at the school board meeting that night. Peabody was a tall, slim, dark-haired man with a smile that would melt most young women. He dressed in a vested suit and tie with shoes that were military shined to a T. Tilde was also tall, but she was plain with long graying hair that was pulled back into a bun at the nape of her neck.

Looking back, George could remember it clearly.

Peabody immediately answered George's knock. "Come in, I have been looking for you."

George stomped the snow off his feet. "Shall I take off my boots?"

"No, that's just fine. Follow me to my bedroom. It happened in here." Peabody stood at the foot of his bed. He lifted the floor-length round tablecloth that covered the round, tall, slim table to reveal the safe. The safe sat under table, which was against the wall. "It looked just like this when I came home. I didn't touch it just in case you wanted to take fingerprints. Tilde, my wife, was gone to play cards. The safe door was pried open," Peabody added. "And so was the back door."

George looked in the safe and saw it was completely empty.

"What was in the safe?" George asked Peabody. "Money or any other important papers?"

"Money. I keep my important papers in a safety deposit box at the bank."

"How much money are we talking about, Peabody?" George asked him.

"A lot." He paused. "I counted it Tuesday night. There was exactly ten thousand eight hundred ninety-six dollars. I know because I always write it down in my ledger and slide it under the doily on the table here." Peabody lifted it, showing George the thin ledger of his records.

"Good Lord." *No one keeps that kind of money at home when we have the First National Bank right on Main Street*, George thought.

"Who knows about your safe and your money?" George had asked him.

"Well, Tilde knows, but she doesn't have the combination. Besides, she was at the card game. No, she would never…I hope you don't think see would, do you?" Peabody curled his face into an "I can't believe you asked that question" look.

George took prints from the safe door and frame, the doorjamb, and the brass rail on the foot of the bed. Carefully, he had taken the Kodak out of its case, and then he took several shots of the robbery scene.

"I have to ask anything and everything that may help me solve who robbed you. Do you pull the shade when you count your money?" he remembered asking Peabody.

"Absolutely." Peabody stuck his chin out in defense. George noted he had never seen this side of the man.

"So no one could see you counting your money?"

"I don't think so."

"My guess is, someone knew you kept money here." George paused. "I'll need your and your wife's prints also. Did you notice anything else in the house disturbed?"

"You need our prints? Why? We didn't rob ourselves."

"For comparison, Mr. Peabody." George sounded slightly disgusted.

"Oh, of course, very well. Tilde, come here, the sheriff needs to take our prints. And no, nothing else was touched as far as I know."

Tilde had appeared in the doorway looking a little nervous. George noticed her hands were shaking. He took Tilde's first and then Peabody's prints. He handed a cloth to the two to clean off the ink stains on their fingers. Finishing the job, George stood up and said, "I'll look around outside for anything unusual. However, it has snowed, which won't be helpful. If you think of anything else, you let me know. I'll check back with you tomorrow. The prints I have are only half or partial. I'll compare these to yours."

George put them in his evidence box in the backpack. "One more question. Why did you wait before calling me?"

"George, I did try to get you ever since I woke this morning. Because it was very late last night, I decided to wait until today. You are a very busy man."

"That's what my wife tells me." George remembered, grinning. "I was here and there this morning. I understand."

Next, George recalled that he let himself out, closed the door, and headed towards the back door, searching for any clues along the porch, down the steps, and over the snowbanks. *Nothing unusual here*, he remembered thinking. He went to the backyard and looked over the spot where the door was broken in to check for splinters or any other clue. The paint was white over a dark green. Some small splinters were lying under the snow on the back porch. He took one and put it in the clue box to take to the office. Next, he looked at the bedroom window. Anyone could see into the room clearly with the blinds up. A closer look revealed the entire room and its contents, even when the lace curtains were drawn.

George had asked himself, who knew that there was money in Peabody's safe? He also wondered why Peabody didn't want his wife to know how much money was in the safe.

George continued to remember how Isabel was in bed with her face turned towards the wall. The ashtray was full of fresh cigarette butts. George emptied them and warmed up the leftover food. While he ate that night, he thought how much his wife had changed in the ten years they had been married. He met her in Lansing at a sheriff and state trooper's convention. She was at the bar in the lounge where he was staying. One look at her beauty, long dark slightly curly hair and snappy eyes, made his whole being jolt into attention. He had not felt that way since the loss of his first wife. They were married within a couple days, via a quick trip to Canada. They returned home a happy couple. She was a hard worker at home and at the school doing maintenance work. She was an excellent cook. He really didn't have any complaints; she was always ready to please him. He thought she was happy because of the way she laughed at their tenth wedding anniversary. That was truly a good sign of her happiness.

George reflected that night after he finished eating, he went to bed. Isabel acted as though she was sleeping. When he reached for her, he convinced her she was very awake.

CHAPTER FIVE

An Experiment

That was a couple days ago. George stomped the snow off his feet before entering. He could smell his dinner come through the door, bringing a smile to his face for the first time since early that morning.

After a comforting meal, he cleaned up and headed to the bedroom. The last thoughts were about who he would see the next day. Stubby had said he last saw Two Shoes at Cedarville Bar sometime Wednesday night. His last thoughts before he fell asleep was to follow this lead in the morning.

Fresh coffee reached his nostrils the next morning. Isabel was humming to herself and preparing breakfast before leaving for work. It took him just a few minutes to clean up and shave. Isabel was leaving out the back door as he entered the kitchen.

"Hey, going already?" George asked.

"Jeanette and I are having coffee and a talk before starting this morning, so I'm taking a few minutes to allow the time."

"I'm sorry about last night, but duty calls, Isabel."

"I realize that, George. Did you get any rest last night?"

"Sure, why?"

"You were talking about all that money and Peabody keeping secrets."

"No kidding? Keep that under your hat, Isabel."

"I know, I know, nothing leaves this house…"

"Have a good day at work." George reached over and kissed her full on the lips.

Isabel smiled and said, "See ya."

George ate and placed the dishes in the sink. He sat at the table and read the latest *Breeze* newspaper, made the bed, and soon was ready to begin the day.

As he read, his mind began thinking of all of Two Shoes' friends and relatives that may lead him to what happened. He jotted their names on a list; he could check with them later. He also wished to talk to the bartender at Cedarville Bar to see if she remembered who all was in that night when Stubby saw Two Shoes there. Witness were more important at this time. He added two more names to the list. He pulled on his overcoat and headed out the door to Cedarville Bar. The air was brisk, but just thinking about getting a lead on the events of the week made George feel better than he had for a couple days. He actually had a spring in his step.

George held his list in one hand as he walked to the garage. His truck was parked in front of the garage. There was no new snow from the night before. He stuffed the list in his inside pocket, backed out to the street, and turned towards the bar.

"Hi, stranger," Bonnie, the bartender, called to him as he entered. "I'm really sorry to hear about your buddy, George. If there's anything I can do to help you through this, just say the word."

"Yes, you can help me. Did you work last Tuesday night?"

Bonnie answered, "Yes, I did. Why?"

"I need to know what happened that night when he was here. I need to know if you can remember who all was here while he was. I also need to know what you saw or heard."

"Whoa, one question at a time, okay?"

"Okay, what time did Two Shoes come in that night?"

"If I recall right, I think it was around seven," Bonnie answered.

"Were there many in at that time?"

Bonnie scratched her head and said, "Just a few. Two Shoes ordered a shot of whiskey and a beer right away."

"Hmm, that's unusual, isn't it?" George asked. "I've never seen him drink hard liquor."

"Yes, if I recall, he doesn't drink whiskey. Just beer. Two Shoes looked around and saw Stubby, his fishing buddy, wave at him, and then he went to the round table at the end of the bar."

"Did Stubby join him?"

"For a few minutes. Then Stubby went to sit with the twins from the hardware at the bar."

"Did you see anything unusual that night that warrants mention?"

"Only that after Two Shoes had a few drinks, he became slightly louder and was telling things that should have been left unsaid."

"Like what?"

"He said he was taking his usual shortcut through the woods, and when he came out near Wendell Peabody's home, he noticed something through the window that made him become curious. So he came closer to see why Peabody's head was even with the windowsill."

Bonnie lowered her voice and came closer to George and continued, "He said he saw the most money he had ever seen in his life all stacked up on the bedroom floor. Peabody was counting it out and marking it down on a slip of paper."

George suspected right away that this was why Two Shoes was murdered.

He asked Bonnie to make a list of all who were in the bar that night while Two Shoes was there. Just from their conversation, he realized that Stubby and the twins were there. He asked her to get it for him no later than the next day. Bonnie agreed.

Looking back, it felt like forever since George had woken that morning with the call about Stubby finding Two Shoes' body. Two days had passed, and George had visited a few of Two Shoes' friends and family with no leads, just hunches. His visit with Bonnie was on hold until she had a list of those who were there on Tuesday night, and he was tired. Finally, after a long day, George arrived home to a dark cabin. Quietly, he sat upon the bed edge and removed his boots, stockings, flannel shirt, and jeans. He slipped under the covers and reached for Isabel.

"Isabel, are you awake?"

"Yes," she said. "You jiggled the bed while undressing."

"How was your day?"

"What do you think? Sweep the floors, mop the floors, scrub the toilets, same old crap. If I didn't need the money to get the things I want, I would just stay home and wait for you to come home when you are ready to."

"Isabel, I need to tell you something. It has been a long day, but we really haven't had a chance to talk, and I really need to tell you this." He hesitated a moment.

"What is so important that it can't wait until tomorrow?" Isabel asked. She swung around, looking at George.

"Stubby found Two Shoes day before yesterday frozen in the ice."

Silence.

"Let's go to sleep, I'm tired." Isabel turned her back with a huff.

George reached over and kissed her on the back. "Let's not do this. We love each other, and that will never change. Let's do something together soon. I miss our happy times. Okay?"

"Uh-huh," she mumbled sleepily.

George lay there wide awake, thinking. His brain wouldn't shut down. Isabel being upset added to his restlessness. So much had happened in his life the past thirteen years. He thought back when he was fresh out of college, a graduate of the 1934 class at Michigan State University. Remembering how he brought his new wife, Beatrice, home from Lansing to live with him on the farm with his family. They stayed with his family while his father and brother helped him build a small cabin in the woods around the corner where they could be alone. It wasn't much, a one-room cabin with a path. The bed sat in the corner where his wife put up a curtain to separate their bedchamber. The fireplace kept them warm in the winter. A long log table sat in front of the fireplace where Beatrice cooked, as it was more convenient for her. A pair of chairs were placed away from the table where the couple sat to read the Bible in the evening.

Ah, so long ago, I should have been there, I should have been there. And now my best buddy... George put his face in the pillow, while his body shook in silent tears. Sleep finally came as well as relief from the grief from loss of two loved ones.

The ring of the telephone woke George the next morning. He answered to find it was his mother.

"I heard the news. I had to call and…George, I know what you are feeling. First, it was Beatrice, your first wife, your child, and now your best friend, Two Shoes."

"Thank you, Mom, for your comforting words."

He took a deep breath and let it out slowly. He knew how lucky he was as not to become an alcoholic, and he was grateful to have Isabel for the past ten years. She wasn't Beatrice, but she had been good for him in many ways.

Isabel walked into the room. "I don't like being alone."

"Let's spend time together today then. What would you like to do?" George asked.

"Can we meet here today after work?" Isabel seemed content with George's question.

"I'll be here." Sitting at the table, George glanced over at Isabel and asked, "Remember when we met?"

"You came down to Lansing for the sheriff's convention. I was hanging around the convention hall, and you 'picked me up.'"

"You were the prettiest thing I had seen for a long time. That long black hair and those snappy eyes, you hooked me on the spot."

"And then we went to Canada and was married the next day," Isabel continued. "It all sounded so romantic to move way up here away from all the city life and be in a quiet peaceful place. But that was ten years ago. It is getting old now. I miss the city where you can go everywhere without having to travel miles and miles to get there."

"What do you say when we get a break, maybe in the spring, we take a trip to Lansing?" George asked her. "Or look up your folks. How does that sound?"

"It sounds good, but I don't want to see my family, none of them."

"Whatever you want, Isabel. I just want you to be happy."

"Let's take a walk," Isabel said with the old childish glint in her eyes she had when they were first married.

"Sure, why not." He was trying to please her; there had been a strain on their marriage for quite a time, and it definitely needed mending. This could ease the pain and help him think clearer.

After work, Isabel saw George waiting as she walked across from the high school. A gentle wind blew from the south; the sky was clear and the sun shining. The temperature was on the rise. They were getting the January thaws, George reminded her. There were puddles of sludge here and there as they walked along the street, holding hands like teenagers. If anyone saw the two, they would say they made a good match. The two were quite tall, slim in figure, and both wore a smile.

If only all the underlying currents of their everyday life's experiences were not threatening. If only George wasn't constantly thinking about Two Shoes' death and the robbery, all the suspicions, questions unanswered, but he knew he needed to enjoy the moment. This day was for Isabel and himself.

Tomorrow he planned to pursue the investigation and question everyone he had put on the list; everyone he suspected.

CHAPTER SIX

A Discovery

The next day, George encouraged Isabel by saying, "I'll clean the dishes and tidy up the kitchen for you."

Isabel looked surprised and smiled as she left for work.

George worried that her unhappiness living in such an area and under the cloud of his occupation would lead to her leaving him. She was so dogmatic about his not being home and never spending time with her. He would try to give her more attention.

It was near time for him to go to the office when the phone rang.

"Hi, George, you have an incoming call from St. Ignace," the operator said.

"Hello?"

"It's Drake. As soon as I called Zimmerman, the pathologist, he started up here. He had a hell of a trip, the weather was wind and snow all the way. He didn't get here until Big Chief came across from Mackinac City yesterday. Stayed at my home and began the work right away. We've completed the autopsy. Are you sitting down?"

"No, what is it?"

"We both believe your man, Two Shoes, was murdered."

"I had a hunch you would tell me that," George said. "How did you come to this conclusion?"

"If he fell, he would have just one wound. His head had three, possibly four, very heavy blows to the skull, leaving cerebral hemorrhaging as well as contusions to other parts of his shoulders and neck. It was impossible to get a definite blood type from the blood sample you gave me. Just Two Shoes.'"

"This changes the course of my investigation. The family wish to do the ceremonial cedar washing before embalmment. When can the family do this to prepare him for a traditional Native American ceremony? You know they have a special way of sending their own to the Great Spirit."

"I know George, and I respect the clan for that. Anytime now. Tomorrow will be okay. I'll call them to let them know. Do you have Lightfoot's phone number?"

"Yes." He reached into his pocket for the tiny notepad with important numbers and said, "It's two thousand eight. And thanks, Drake, I need to get right on this. Since the thaw yesterday, I need to check the area outdoors at the robbery last Wednesday night and swing around to the murder scene right after that. There may be a connection between the robbery and the murder. It's just too coincidental. The biggest case I've had so far, not to mention cats in a tree and a few bar fights," George added to keep things light.

"Hey, let me know if I can do anything, George. I know how you must be feeling right now. I remember just a few years ago when Beatrice passed away, you went through a lot then, and now your lifelong friend. I'm sorry. But like I said, I'll be ready to help with the investigation if you need me or the boys from over this way."

"Thanks, Drake, I appreciate your offer," answered George.

As George hung up the phone, he recalled the last time he talked to Two Shoes.

They were in the Cedarville Bar. Two Shoes was drinking a Budweiser beer, which he acquired the taste for while he was in the Army.

"Did I ever tell you the story about the 'green horn' in the woods with the lumberjacks?" George asked.

"No, but I know you're going to tell me."

"Well," George began, "It seems the crew sent the 'green horn' back to the camp to get a 'cant hook.' The 'green horn' didn't know what it was, so he went to the cook's shack. 'Could you tell me where

I can find a cant hook?' The cook said, 'Out in the barn, there's an ox that has been dehorned. He can't hook.'"

Two Shoes gently punched George in the arm, and they both laughed.

As their laughter subsided, George asked, "How's the trapping going?"

"Oh, fairly good, I have had some getaway, though. I can tell there was a fox in the trap by the fur and blood left there, but no pelt."

"The fox didn't chew his leg off to get out?"

"No trace of that."

A cool chill came over the room. Two Shoes looked up at the same time as most of the people in the bar. The huge shadow of Pierre Bouchard had entered. He stood at the door for a few seconds and found a seat away from the crowd. He was not a man to see soap more than once a year in the spring.

Two Shoes had looked at Bouchard with disdain and said, "I believe Pierre is taking my pelts. I can't prove it, but like I told you, I have had fox and beaver in my traps. The tracks show me this, but they're always empty."

"There has to be a way to catch him, possibly you could discreetly follow him."

"Possibly."

George reflected, *I'll always remember that conversation.* He reached for the list and added Pierre Bouchard's name. There had to be a correlation between the robbery and the murder; George's hunch was valid. But who? Why?

George grabbed his coat and hat and drove over to Peabody's home. Tilde answered the door in a housedress with a lace-trimmed apron over it.

"Tilde, I'd like to check again for any clues to your robbery. I have evidence that should be followed up."

"Go ahead and do your job. If you need to come in, you're welcome."

"I'll start in the house first and then outdoors and grounds. Since the thaw, something may show up."

He quickly repeated his search from last week when Peabody called him about the robbery. He went back to the bedroom. He looked all around. The bed was in the same position, dresser and safe with the door still open, under the round table sitting to the wall at the foot of the bed with walking room in between. The table had previously housed the safe below it under the floor-length tablecloth. He walked closer towards the safe. It was here he noticed a scent of a musky earthy odor. He looked toward the closet, opened it, and sniffed. No, it wasn't the closet. He stepped back towards the end of the bed and sniffed inside the safe. The musky smell came from the safe. He jotted something on his pad and decided to go to the outside of the house where he hoped to come up with something of interest, something he may have missed on his previous visit. With the thaw, more tiny wood fragments from the break-in were on the back porch. Looking very closely, he discovered more almost minute fragments of white and green paint on the back steps.

He could clearly see where he walked out around the house previously. Suddenly, something caught his eye. Looking down, he could see a few fine wood fragments and paint flecks both white and green. There was a strange track or print in the snow. It looked like a crow print but somewhat larger and only one. He shook his head.

George knocked again on the back door. Mrs. Peabody answered, "What is it, George?"

"Have you seen a crow around here lately?" *That was a dumb question. When do you see a one-footed crow?* he thought. It could be something similar but not a crow.

"Not that I can recall," she answered. "Why?"

George answered, "Thank you, Tilde. I'll let you or your husband know what I find out. I'd like to talk to him when he returns from the principal's office at school today."

George wanted to check out the murder scene once more before the snow completely melted the evidence, or it snowed again and covered everything again.

Near the sheriff office door, George reached down and drew three lines in the shape of a crow track. *I'll check this later this afternoon to see if it gets bigger.*

As George stepped into the entry, he saw Maria at her desk in the printing office. Her beautiful curly red hair looked especially good today with the Kelly green dress she wore. "Hey, Marie, do you have plans for lunch?" George asked as he briefly glanced into the press office.

"I brought my own, but I have enough for you too, if you like toast and fried egg."

"Sounds good to me. Do you have hot coffee?"

"I have the pot on over there in the corner. I use the hot plate to make it in my aluminum coffeepot."

"I thought I smelled it." George smiled at her. "Fact is, I knew you did have coffee too."

"Here have a seat." She cleared the papers off the seat near her desk. "How's the investigation going?"

"Working hard on it. No big leads yet." He bit into his sandwich, reached to the coffee mug, and swallowed a long drink.

"Sure has been warm, the snow is melting. Have you heard when the funeral will be held?"

"I know that Two Shoes is at the funeral parlor being embalmed. I was told the elders went over and washed him with the cedar bath, a ritual purification procedure, before he would be embalmed. Two Shoes will be brought to the community hall where he can be viewed for four days. The fire keeper will begin the fire today and keep it going for that period. The funeral will be held on the fourth day."

"So that would be on Saturday afternoon?" Marie was looking at the calendar that hung directly below the oak Ingraham pendulum clock.

"Possibly. I'll check to make sure." He finished the last bite and wadded up the wax paper and tossed it into the wastebasket.

"That sandwich really hit the spot. Thank you for sharing it with me. It was a very nice lunch, and I enjoyed your company, Marie."

"What are you going to do now?"

"I'll need to go out to the murder scene just to check for any other clues, evidence, anything to solve who did this."

As he was leaving the office, George spotted Lightfoot parking his vehicle. His car had an emblem on it saying, "Mackinac County Chippewa Tribal Affairs."

"New emblem?" George pointed to the car door.

"Ya, white man calls the Ojibwa, Chippewa."

George remembered he asked Lightfoot to help with the investigation.

"You're just the guy I want to see. I wanted to call you before this, but now that I've heard from the coroner, I really need to talk to you. I got word earlier this morning that Two Shoes was murdered. I think I know why, and I'm definitely going to need your help."

"Drake called to let us know we could come over to do the cedar bath, and two elders and I went. Drake didn't tell us anything. He was murdered? It wasn't an accident?" Lightfoot's face froze in a determined expression. White man had done things like this and got away with it many times in the past. He was determined to find the culprit.

"Seriously, there are too many issues here, and I'm ready for you to join me. Your input is good since Two Shoes is Native American. You can convince his people he is getting a fair investigation. With you being with me, it will work out fine. That should be reason enough. What do you say?"

The two had walked back out to the street, and Lightfoot leaned against his car, holding his chin. George looked seriously into his face. Lightfoot remained silent.

George knew this was serious, very serious. Two Shoes was a Native American, a war hero, and well liked in the community; it shouldn't have happened to him. Having Lightfoot with him would help George from being tempted to be one-sided with his decisions. Even though he loved his friend, the peer pressure would make him struggle slightly, and Lightfoot's views mingled with George's would help make a more accurate decision in the investigation. This was a rural region where murder was a rare event.

"I need you, Lightfoot, for many reasons mainly because of the prejudices against the Native Americans. Two Shoes' family and the tribe will need to know exactly how we conduct the investigation and bring justice to the perpetrator."

"I agree." Lightfoot finally made a sign to answer George's plea. "You do need this help. I'll join you in the search of my cousin's murderer. This is more than routine for me, it's personal." Lightfoot stood up straight, away from his car.

George reached into his pocket, pulled out a paper, and said, "Let's start with the list of people I received from Bonnie, which includes all who were at the bar last Tuesday. Then we will dig into other possibilities. I have it here, let's see." George checked the list. "My guess is we should start with Pierre Bouchard because Two Shoes didn't trust him. He believed that Bouchard was stealing his traps and pelts. Pierre could have heard Two Shoes that night when the information about Peabody's money was talked about. I believe Pierre is out on the trapline along Pine River. If he isn't there, we can swing around towards the swamp where he claimed traps and pelts for his own near the old St. Ignace road."

"What are you saying? I need to catch up. What was this about Peabody and money?"

"It seems Two Shoes was talking about seeing Peabody counting his money. I don't have all the facts yet, but as we investigate, I'm sure we will hear more."

"So you believe this is the connection with Two Shoes' death?" Lightfoot asked.

"Possibly. Yes, it has to because it's too coincidental that two crimes were committed in such a short time frame. There has to be a connection." While he talked to Lightfoot, he looked at the snow at the corner of the building and smiled to himself.

"I did a little experiment here, made tracks in the snow to see if they would get bigger after the thaw this afternoon. They do."

CHAPTER SEVEN

Investigation Begins

Lightfoot cleared his throat and stated, "I'd like to go out to the murder scene to see if any blood was uncovered today."

"That's where I saw the track on the day of the discovery. I found one similar to it in the backyard at Peabody's home after the robbery. Things are beginning to pull together."

"Hop in, we can head there first." George opened his truck door while Lightfoot reached the passenger side and seated himself.

George drove over to Smith's Landing, parked his truck, and followed the snow path across the yard to the ice. The melt revealed more than he had expected. There was a large area where blood was on the ice, leaving a trail all the way to the fishing hole.

Blood was in a puddle near the other print—a crow type print.

"Looks like he was hit here near this puddle and dragged over to the trench," Lightfoot said.

"Yes, where he was shoved or pulled into the water. Had to be near dead because it appeared that he grabbed the ice just as he entered the frigid water," George added.

"The shock of being hit plus the subzero water would do anyone in," Lightfoot concluded.

"I believe the tracks looking like a single crow track was made with the murder weapon," George said as they walked back across the ice to the truck.

"Could be."

They headed west to Hessel and then due north on Three Mile to Dixie Highway west. Driving out the old trail, the deer were moving. The deer crossed the road to get a drink from Lake Huron where the thaw brought extra water to drink. The snow-covered gravel road slowed him down as well. This made it impossible for George to drive more than forty-five miles per hour. "I'm glad it isn't spring. The melted snow and ice always turns this road to mud and gravel. It's almost impossible to travel at that time."

"It sure was a bugger last spring. I remember how I was stuck and walked to get help to get the stuck vehicle out," Lightfoot said.

They passed Pontchartrain Trail knowing it was a narrow path that was mainly used to take out timber as well as cedar posts north to Dixie Highway, which was also called M-134, leading George and Lightfoot west to Mackinaw Trail. They crossed Pine River, and a few miles later, George turned south onto Mackinaw Trail with its many curves through pine trees and cedars. They went over Carp River on down nearer to St. Ignace, where there were more cedar and pines with a few poplar and birch trees through which a brief glimpse of Lake Huron was revealed. Finally, they viewed the bay with Mackinaw Island in the background as they continued south. They turned west up the hill, away from the water's edge, a couple blocks where they planned to visit the local undertaker who covered as coroner as well.

The yellow three-story colonial style home stood in magnificent centennial glory. The coroner lived in the back and upstairs. The front of the first floor was the showing and funeral quarters, while the embalming and autopsies were done in the huge basement.

A paved sidewalk led to the east entrance lined with trees on either side. Lightfoot and George rang the doorbell and entered through beveled glass double doors leading into a foyer where they took the stairs to the basement.

"Hope the lab isn't too busy so we can get on our way," Lightfoot said.

"All I need to do is see the fingerprints' report. After that, we'll leave."

"Good."

Drake sat in his oak rocking chair. The small room kept his supplies, a filing cabinet and desk. There were two straight back oak chairs near the door. The adjoining room had curtained French doors dividing the two rooms. One of the doors was ajar, where George could see a narrow table where Drake did autopsies, along with supply closets, a sink with a metal counter and drawers and metal cupboards beneath them. A microscope and other equipment were lined up on the counter.

Drake stood up and shook hands with both of the men.

"Come on in, boys. Always good to see a live body where I do my handiwork. Take a seat." He motioned to the two straight chairs. "What can I do for you today? I can guess it's something about Two Shoes."

"I'm wondering about the fingerprint report from the robbery I submitted. Did you find anything about whom they belong to?"

"George, there are so few half and smudged prints. I'm sorry I have nothing on record that matches. Really, I'm not the one who usually does this. I took them to the county sheriff's office, hoping to find something. They sent the report with me knowing you were coming in. As you can see, they didn't find anything."

"I hope someday we will be able to check blood types and fingerprints with a more proficient method to help solve murders like this," George said, disappointed.

"In time, all in time," Drake said as he puffed on his curved pipe and watched the two turn to climb the steps and leave.

A serious search began for the murderer from that moment. George was silently thinking, *He knew Two Shoes had been bludgeoned and left for dead. The blood trail proved this. And since he wasn't dead, he gripped the edge with one hand in the throb of his last heartbeat.*

George looked at Lightfoot and said, "I can't help thinking how Two Shoes grasped the edge of the ice as he sunk into the icy water."

Lightfoot added, "The murderer could have made it look like he fell in, hit his head, and struggled to get out."

George nodded his head and said, "True."

Once on the old Mackinaw Trail again, they quickly found a place to park the truck. Lightfoot went one way along the river, looking for tracks, while George went the other.

"Fresh tracks over here," George called to Lightfoot. Within minutes, Lightfoot joined George, and they inched their way along the marked trail. Pierre's foot tracks were large and deep along the trapping trail. Pine River turned and circled north off the main road. Finding fresh footsteps, which headed in a direction away from where they started, encouraged the two men onward. Soon Lightfoot touched George on the arm and put his finger to his lip.

"I hear him muttering about something or to someone," he whispered. Then he raised his hand for George to stop. He pointed his finger across where Pierre Bouchard was kneeling over a trap. Pierre's rifle was resting against a stump nearby. The two looked around to see if there was anyone with Pierre. A sense of forewarning brought Pierre around with a rifle barrel pointing straight into George's face.

"What do you want?" Pierre growled.

George stepped back and raised his hands. "Hold on, Pierre. Lightfoot here, and I have to talk to you. Thought you'd be here somewhere along the trapline."

"What you need to talk about?" Pierre growled.

"Two Shoes has been murdered. Have you heard anything about it?"

"Been too busy doing my pelts, checking traps, and resetting them to get to town or talk to anyone. How did he get murdered?"

"He was found in his ice hole frozen stiff, on Les Cheneaux Channel."

"Well, you got the wrong man. I didn't do it!"

"What about you taking his pelts?" George asked.

"Did he accuse me of doing that?"

"He suspected and also said he couldn't trust you and that he believed you were dishonest."

Pierre's face became dark red, veins bulging in his neck and forehead. "I tell you who's dishonest, the Sheppard twins. They cheated me when I bought my traps!" He came closer to George and looked straight into his face. "I did not kill Two Shoes!"

"Can you prove it?" Lightfoot asked.

Lightfoot stepped even closer to Pierre and looked into his eyes. "And I tell you, Pierre Bouchard, for your sake, I hope you are telling the truth. He was one of our people and loved by many." He stepped away and, for a moment, looked straight ahead.

That was a lot of words for a man who just doesn't talk much, George thought. "Pierre, just for the record, where were you Friday afternoon and evening?" George asked.

"I came in from the trapline, put away my pelts, and went to the Cedarville Bar for a drink."

"So you were in the vicinity of Les Cheneaux Channel?"

"No, I wasn't anywhere near the channel. I was at the Cedarville Bar."

"Have you ever had thoughts of harming Two Shoes?"

"Why should I? All I want in life is to survive. I'm no different than most people who live in this area."

"So you survive by taking pelts from other trappers, including Two Shoes'?" Lightfoot asked Pierre.

"I tell you already 'bout that. I am honest, hardworking man," Pierre said in broken English.

"Okay, get on with your work," George said.

"I'll be taking care of Two Shoes traps until after the burial ceremony. Permission from Chief," Lightfoot said.

"I get it, stay away from dem," Pierre commented.

Lightfoot looked directly at Pierre Bouchard and said one word: "Right."

It took a half hour for George and Lightfoot to work their way back through the swampy cedar and birch-laden trail to the truck. George started the truck and headed eastward towards Cedarville.

"Where to next, boss?" asked Lightfoot.

"I'm not your boss. We're in this together, remember?"

CHAPTER EIGHT

The Shepherd Twins

Lightfoot looked at Bonnie's list and saw the Sheppard twins' name on it. "We probably should stop in at Sheppard's Hardware Store and talk to the boys." Lightfoot paused. "For me, that will be harder. I have trouble talking to those who think they are better than our kind," Lightfoot said.

"Don't feel that way Lightfoot, you are better than some and more to me."

"I never thought any different with you, George, but you are an exception to the rule."

The red brick hardware store stood on the south side of the street across the street from the sheriff's office. It backed against the Cedarville Bay. The hardware entrance door receded four feet in where the two front windows and side windows displayed their supplies on both sides. You could easily see the latest wringer washer, woven wicker clothes' baskets, and clothespins displayed in one of the windows, while a wheelbarrow, a few lawn tools, and a reel push lawn mower were in the other.

Upon entering, Lightfoot and George saw Gilbert up on the ladder restocking his many supplies and part bins from the floor to the ceiling. The ladder was on a track with pulleys, so it easily followed the track on the ceiling from one end of the store to the other. The bins were filled with bolts, nuts, tacks, and nails of all sizes. There were small parts and fittings for pipes made of brass, copper, and steel. On the opposite wall, every kind of paint, varnish, and all the accessories needed, brushes, thinner, stirrers, were stacked on shelves to the ceiling. A ladder on tracks worked the same way to reach the paint and varnish stock.

A huge crank style National Cash Register was in the center of the room near the double doorway leading customers to the west half of the store. There you could find pots and pans, Maytag wringer washers, reel-type push lawn mowers, toasters, and West Clock windup alarm clocks of various sizes. Bradbury pocket watches were sold at the cash register counter. The window screen and glass was in the back with the page wire and barbed wire, and a barrel of wheel grease stood at the back door. Binder twine could also be purchased there.

George purchased all his small hand tools here.

"Hello, George, how are you doing today?" Gilbert looked at Lightfoot and nodded.

"Well, Gilbert, we need to talk to you about something. Is Wilber here?"

"Sure, he's in the back fixing a broken window for a customer."

"Good, could you have him cover while you come across to my office for a few minutes?"

"No customers here today, I'm sure he can. Wilber!"

Wilber came out wiping his hands. "What is it?"

"I need to go with George for a few minutes."

"Okay." Wilbert looked puzzled and curious. Nodding assurance, the trio left, walking across the slushy snow and ice-covered street.

George saw Maria through the glass window panes in her news office. Her head was lowered at her desk, looking busy, when the three entered the sheriff's office across the hall. The double-paned glass made his office soundproof, yet it was easy to look across and see who went in and out. He could see her pendulum clock ticking back and forth. It showed three thirty.

George took the chair behind his large old oak desk, which was originally old man Sutherlands. Mr. Sutherland took pleasure from buying the very best, and this desk would last for another one hundred years. Lightfoot took the chair to the right near the woodstove. He opened the door to the stove and poked the coals, stirring them up, and then placed a log on them to warm the office up. Gilbert Sheppard took the chair to the left, in front of and facing George. The walls were blank with the exception of a huge framed picture of Abraham Lincoln, which hung on the wall behind George's desk. Wilbert thought Lincoln looked sternly into his eyes and shivered. Lightfoot leaned back and swung his chair as he looked directly at Gilbert as well as George.

"Gilbert, I'm going to start with a straight question. You probably already heard that Two Shoes was murdered. He was discovered early Saturday morning. My question is, do you know anything about it?"

"So, he really was murdered?" Gilbert rubbed under his nose with his finger, looked at the wall above Abe, and began to talk. "I heard a few rumors. Some said he slipped and fell into his fishing trench. I knew Two Shoes drank. Sometimes he drank quite a lot, but he always seemed to be in complete control of his faculties. I wondered when I was told that. He could have stumbled over a piece of ice and fell in. The ice is rough, and this could happen to anyone. Maybe he stumbled to get away from someone who was threatening him. I don't know. I'm going to miss him. Most people liked him. I liked him. I never had a problem with him. He always paid his bill. Even when he was gone overseas, I held the bill his parents used on charges. When he came back, he paid it to date."

"I appreciate your honesty. That's a good report, and it's quite thorough. Do you know of any reason why he was murdered?" George looked at him and then at Lightfoot. "Like, did you hear anything in the past week that would give you an idea as to why he was murdered?"

"I can't recall…maybe…but I'm not sure." Gilbert said.

Lightfoot stood up. "Not sure what?"

Gilbert leaned back and looked up at Lightfoot with fear in his eyes. "I think I heard something about Peabody and money, but I only heard parts of it. I can't tell you any more than that. I'm not sure, I just don't know."

"What did you hear? When and who told you?" George asked.

"I think I heard Two Shoes say he saw a lot of money."

"When?"

"Tuesday night."

"Where?"

"At Cedarville Bar."

"You haven't heard anything else since then? Even now after the murder?" George asked Gilbert.

"Stubby told us about how he found Two Shoes."

Stubby again, always did talk too much, George thought. "What did he tell you?"

"Just that you and Smith and he pulled Two Shoes' body out of Les Cheneaux Channel."

"How did you feel when he told you this?"

Gilbert looked down at the floor, readjusted himself, sat more upright, having built a little more self-confidence, and then said, "I found it appalling and thought it was a bad way to go. I wondered how it happened. Probably all these thoughts have held others who also cared for him. Then I asked, why? Why did this happen? I wish I knew, but I don't. At first, I felt it was an accident, and then when I heard he might have been murdered, I believed he was fighting for his life." Gilbert scuffed his shoe across the wide pine floorboards and then looked back to George.

"He may have. Only the murderer and Two Shoes know," George said. Then he added, "And God. He knows."

Gilbert stood up and gripped his hat in his hands, his eyes holding a sad appearance, perhaps a worried look. "Is that all you need?" he asked.

"Yes, you may go. Lightfoot, will you accompany Gilbert and bring back Wilber?"

"That won't be necessary, George. I'll send him directly."

"I know you mean well, but if not Lightfoot, I will go along with you. These are proper procedures in an investigation, especially how I handle it."

"I'll go with Gilbert and get Wilber, George."

Lightfoot followed him to the hardware store where he looked for Wilber. He was standing at the register in the middle of the hardware store.

Lightfoot looked at Wilber. "It's your turn, Wilber, ready?"

George watched from the entrance where he stood with the heavy double oak door open. He saw Gilbert enter, and seconds later, Wilber came out. He was the smaller of the twins and walked with a swagger. He shuffled his feet through the ice and snow, crossing Bay Side Street to George's office. George was seated and waited as they entered down the hall. Wilber looked nervously into the news office and then towards the sheriff's office where he found George's door ajar.

"Come on in, Wilber. Take a seat," George said as he gestured towards the empty seat in front of the desk. Wilber looked at George, then at Lightfoot as he closed the office door, and across at Marie through the glass-divided hallway. He took off his cap and jacket and sat down.

"What's this all about anyway, George?" Wilber included Lightfoot as he glanced his way. "She can't hear what we talk about, can she?"

"No, she can't. To come right out with it, Wilber, I am investigating the death and murder of Two Shoes. Where were you last Friday afternoon up until dark?"

"We kept the store open until eight o'clock as usual on the weekend. Both Gilbert and me and my wife came in to help from five to eight."

"Well, that puts you and your brother in the clear up until eight. Can you tell me what you did after you left the hardware store? Is there anything else you know about this?"

Wilber fidgeted in his chair while George and Lightfoot waited for an answer. Wilber unbuttoned his woolen shirt, swallowed, cleared his throat, and began to talk.

"Here's what I know. I did hear Two Shoes talking on Tuesday night. Not all of it but enough to know there was a safe full of money in Peabody's house. And I'll add that Two Shoes saw it because I

51

heard him telling Stubby, and it was loud enough that everyone could hear him."

George nodded.

"It's been a rough year at the store. With the war ending, things slumped. The first year, business wasn't bad. Tourists held things together through the summer, and then the rough long winter came with very little business. The second year began to pick up when tourists returned. Business began to pick up when spring crops and much-needed supplies for summer brought the locals back for business, plus the wealthy islanders added to our business also. Locals need our stock when it is necessary, you know, repairs, parts, or purchasing for Christmas in the fall."

"True, I try to get my tools and parts at your store," George said.

"Business has been pretty slow. Personally, our families went without."

"I'm sorry to hear that," George said.

"We haven't restocked our shelves and will not until spring. Gilbert wasn't stocking the bins. He was checking to see how low the stock was getting."

Wilber stopped a minute and said, "Tempted? I sure was, but I promise you I did not think for more than a fleeting second about all that money. My brother and I are not that type. We always go and have a beer or two before going home, but we both agreed this will cease or, at least, slow down until spring."

"I understand what you mean. Cutting back a little may pull you through until spring if you purchase less stock."

"That's right." Wilber stood up and buttoned his coat. "Is there anything else you wish to ask me?"

"Not right now but perhaps in the future." George also stood up.

"Well, boys, I sure hope you can find the culprit who did this. Two Shoes was a truly honest customer who stood behind his word. We will miss him."

"Thank you for being candid, Wilber. So you are saying you don't know anything about the robbery? You didn't see anything strange or unusual? Like Wednesday night, the night of the robbery, or anything Friday afternoon or evening?" Lightfoot added to the questioning.

Wilber looked down at his feet and shuffled them. "Nope, I sure didn't."

George looked across the street, seeing a customer enter.

"Can't say I did. We haven't gone to the bar since last Tuesday."

"Well, okay. I guess that is all I will ask for now. If your memory gets any better, give us a call."

"Sure will." Wilber was ready to leave. "I better get back and help my brother finish the inventory."

"Good day."

Lightfoot and George heard the office door shut as Wilbur's feet shuffled down the hall to the entrance door and the heavy slam of the oak door as it closed. They knew he was gone.

Lightfoot immediately said, "What was that stall before he said anything about if he saw anything strange or unusual?"

"So you noticed. Yah, he did stall, looked at his feet. There is something else. Why am I remembering this same gesture? Someone else did this?" George stopped and looked up. "Ah! It was Peabody when I asked him if there was anything else in the safe. He's hiding something too. I noticed you scribbled down what Pierre said, and I thank you. I recorded the twins' answers to my questions in my journal, and I noticed you wrote them also. We can compare notes tomorrow. Time to go home and get some rest."

"So, tomorrow we're going over to talk to Bonnie? She must know something more than the list of patrons she supplied," Lightfoot asked and partially answered.

"That was the plan until I recalled that Two Shoes told Stubby that night about the money. Remember Pierre said they sat together, Two Shoes and Stubby, when he overheard Two Shoes as he talked loudly about it. So, the thought was, why didn't Stubby tell me about it? He actually said he lost interest in fishing and then left the murder scene without offering anything. Just now, the twins let us know the same story. We need to talk to Stubby."

"You're right. See you in the morning."

CHAPTER NINE

Stubby, a Tall Swede

The night brought cold winds from the northwest, which cooled off the small cabin. When George woke abruptly, he noticed his alarm clock at 2:30 am. He got up to restock the woodstove. The frigid floor touched his bare feet. When he returned to the bed, he noticed Isabel still slept soundly, even though the stove door clanked when he shut it. The warmth of the bed was more than welcome. The heavy quilts were still warm. He lay for a while, thinking about what he may discover the next day. He remembered the reactions to questions he asked as well as the answers that each twin said that day. As the words circled around over and over in his mind, he became drowsy again. His last thoughts were that he hoped he wouldn't talk out loud in his sleep again and disturb Isabel.

In his office, George waited for Lightfoot. He arrived later than expected. "Hey, Lightfoot, everything okay?"

"Yes, it took a little longer to thaw this morning." He grinned. "The thermometer set on thirty degrees below."

"I didn't look, but my nostrils stuck fast when I took my first breath as I headed out to the truck. Stubby agreed to come over here to the office. He should arrive anytime now."

"Hmm, maybe he don't want his sweetheart to hear."

"Possible."

About then, the sound of feet stomping off snow came from the foyer, and heavy footsteps in the hallway reached their ears as Stubby filled the doorway. He had to duck down to enter the office.

"Good morning, Stubby. Come in, sit down here." George gestured to the seat in front of the huge oak desk. Lightfoot sat at an angle from the desk where he warmed himself near the woodstove.

Placed on the desk was a fresh notepad and pen. George had refilled it with script ink from his supply from the inkwell on the desk. "Okay, Stubby, will you tell me your full given name?"

"Tage Johansen, pronounced 'Tag,' which rhymes with 'bog.'"

"Spell it, Stubby."

"T-A-G-E."

"Thanks." George wrote it down and then lay down the pen, crossed his arms, and leaned backward in his swivel desk chair. "Tell me, Tage, everything you know about Two Shoes, starting from the last time you talked to him."

Stubby frowned a bit, thinking back, and then began, "It was earlier last week that I was in Cedarville Bar. Two Shoes joined me when he came in. Ya know, we are fishing buddies."

George glanced at Lightfoot, grinned, and nodded while Stumpy cleared his throat and continued, "He had a couple beers and then began talking. He seemed excited about something. He said he usually took a short cut from his folks' cabin through the woods and cedars when the snow wasn't too deep to save time on his way to the bar. On a windy night, the cedars protected him from the wind. This wasn't the first time he told me this, but nevertheless, he continued by saying he noticed the light on in Peabody's bedroom. He didn't know it was his bedroom until he came closer to the house and saw a bed with a flowered chenille spread over it. He was curious because Peabody or someone's head was level with the sill of the window. As he crept closer, he realized it was Peabody kneeling. The green shade was up, so he said he could see clearly through the laced curtains. Since Peabody was on his knees and wasn't praying, he figured he'd get closer and get a better look.

"Then Two Shoes looked me straight in the face and said, 'You'll never guess what I saw, Stubby. Peabody had a pile of green money stacked all around him. He smelled it and had a faraway look on his face. I noticed a couple more things in the safe, but I'm not sure what they were.' And that's all he told me."

"That's it?" George asked. "Think, Stubby, did he appear to be holding anything back?"

"No, he didn't. Well, if he was holding anything back, he sure concealed it."

"Could you tell if anyone appeared to hear what he told you?"

"Don't put words in my mouth, George. What I saw or think I saw is not relevant here. I won't commit myself in any way. It only makes sense to tell you the facts and not what I think."

"So, let's go through this again. You were sitting at a table alone when Two Shoes came in. He joined you, drank a couple beers, and then began to tell you what he saw at Peabody's home. Right?"

"Right."

"Who else was there?"

"The twins from the hardware store across the street. They sat up at the bar, talking to Bonnie. Let's see. I think Pierre Bouchard sat along the wall away from us, you know, near the roller piano. Then there was a couple strangers sitting next to us at a table, and a couple of the regulars sat at the bar near the twins. You know that farmer, Gus, out west of town on Swede Road and his cousin, Pete? He must have stopped by and picked him up on his way into town. Jeffery Beacom was there too, and he never sits for very long anywhere. Then there was Sally, the cook. She sat near the kitchen at the end of the bar. It was kinda slow, bein' the middle of the week."

"Do you know anything about the strangers? Have you seen them before? Have you ever spoken to them? What do they look like? Anything you can remember will help."

"Well, you were there, weren't you?"

"No, I wasn't, Stubby. That was the night I had to be somewhere else."

George quickly jotted down the list: the twins, two strangers, Sally the cook, Gus and Pete, Pierre, Stubby, and Two Shoes, according to Stubby. And Bonnie. "Lightfoot, do you have anything you want to ask Stubby before he leaves?"

56

"Just one thing. Why did you think George was there?"

"I dunno...'cause he usually is, at least, as I recall."

George saw that Stubby was slightly irritated over Lightfoot's question; he did have another question to ask. He waited for his response during the time he watched for any gestures or remarks or facial expression and then said, "Stubby, one last question. Where were you on Friday night?"

"What do you need to know this for?"

"Well, just curious. Were you home or out for a while?"

"I was home."

"Are you sure?"

"Let me think, last Friday, I did go get a haircut in the afternoon and then stopped by the bar for a drink."

"Just one?"

"Yes, I was home by dark. The wind had picked up, and that promised worse weather as the evening progressed."

"So you were out on Friday evening?"

"I guess you could say that."

"Did you see anyone else while you were out?"

"Here we go again. Yes, I saw Rob the barber, Bonnie the bartender, Wilbert, and passed a man in a black hooded sweater on my way home."

"Can you describe this person? Tall? Short? Slim? Fat? Walks with a swagger or swiftly?"

"He was shorter than me, slim, seemed to walk normal, maybe a little in a hurry."

"What time was that?"

"It was already dark." He paused. "Ya, after dark."

"Okay, Stubby, that's all for now. Thanks for coming in. You've been very helpful."

Stubby had a surprised look on his face. He turned toward the door and left.

CHAPTER TEN

A Talk with Bonnie Dickenson, the Barmaid

The outside door slammed shut as Stubby left. George and Lightfoot had to chuckle. Stubby was not sure of anything. It proved to the guys that he was either hiding something or worried about being so close to what happened. They believed his fear of being in trouble made his stomach gnaw.

"You sure you weren't there George?" Lightfoot laughed again.

"Well, I'm pretty sure. That's the night I went to sleep early because I didn't sleep well the night before. You see, I had gone out to see the folks that afternoon and arrived home later than usual. Isabel was a little irritated or restless she kept pacing the floor and couldn't sit for even a minute. So I ate the supper that she kept warm on the cook range, cleaned up, read the Bible for a short while, and then we went to bed. I tried to sleep. I tossed and turned all night, finally getting a couple hours in before five when we got up."

"Just teasing you. That Stubby…" Lightfoot shook his head and chuckled. "He's a mess."

George joined him, laughing.

"Let's go over to talk to Bonnie. She may have time now that the noon rush is over," Lightfoot added.

"Good idea. She may know who the two strange men were. The ones who were in the bar on Tuesday night."

"Ah! Yes, Stubby mentioned them," Lightfoot added.

"It seems they were sitting alone that night, you know, Tuesday, and so far everyone said Two Shoes loudly told his story."

They left the newspaper building and walked west down Bay Street two doors over and across to Cedarville Bar. The one-story building sat back from the street, near the water. Many boaters came in off the bay in the summer months from the dock and in the back door. During winter, the back door was locked, and only the side door on the east wall was used.

They found only one customer who was leaving as they entered and Stubby sitting at the bar puffing on his cigar as he drank a mug of beer. The dark-as-usual bar was dimly lit with only candles at each table.

"Hi, guys, want a beer?" Bonnie asked.

Stubby tipped his glass and gulped the remaining beer, slammed the glass down on the bar, and left, tipping his hat at the two as he passed them.

"Sounds good. Make mine what's on tap, and Robert Lightfoot wants?"

"I'll have the same."

"Bring one for you too, Bonnie. We want you to join us for a talk."

"You, guys, aren't going to sweet-talk me, are you?"

"No, Bonnie, this is serious. We need to ask you a few questions. We promise to let you go if a customer comes in."

Bonnie pulled a chair from the table next and set two beers before the two and a Coca Cola drink at her spot. "What do you want to talk about?"

"Did you hear Two Shoes talking here on Tuesday night?"

"As a matter of fact, I did, but as usual, I keep everything to myself. Remember I told you this, but Lightfoot wasn't here that day, so I understand why you are asking."

"What did you hear?"

"I heard what everyone here that night heard, and I think you know without my filling in the details."

George cleared his throat and said, "That brings me to the second question. Did you see Two Shoes since Tuesday night, at any time or day before Saturday?"

"No, he wasn't in while I was on shift, and I worked every shift this week."

"Have you heard anything else about this happening?"

"Just gossip."

"I should hear your true version of what you saw on Tuesday night," George said.

She began to tell about Two Shoes but didn't seem to know more than what Stubby had told them. Her list of men were the same. She finalized that she kept her personal opinion out, unless they wanted to hear it.

George remained professional and began definite questions that pertained to fact only.

"Bonnie, do you know the names of the two men who were fishing this past week? The ones who were in Tuesday night when Two Shoes talked about the money he saw?"

"The strangers were in that night and every night until Saturday. I was told they went home sometime Saturday or early Sunday morning."

"Do you know their names?"

"No, I don't. Wait, one called the other Sam."

"Bonnie, will you give me a description of the two as best you can? This is important because you probably were the only one who saw them more than anyone here."

"Sam was the taller of the two. They both were slightly overweight, wore expensive outer wear, and they appeared to be laborers because they had rough hands."

"That's it?"

She rubbed the perspiration off her brow with her soiled apron and said, "That's all I know."

"Have you heard anything else that sounded unusual in the past six days?"

"Only bits and pieces."

Lightfoot was looking down, writing notes of the conversation. Then someone came through the door. Bonnie stood up, and the conversation came to a halt. It was "business as usual" for her.

Lightfoot and George drank up the beer and said they would ask around about the men tomorrow. George had to return to the office. "I'll see you early tomorrow," he said. He then looked at the bartender as he called to her, "Thanks for your help, Bonnie."

Bonnie said, "You're most welcome."

"Strange, she clammed up when the customer came in," Lightfoot said.

"True, but she probably wanted to keep everyone from knowing what we were talking about. It helps me to believe she may have nothing to do with foul play. She's a straight shooter."

"People talk, don't they? Well, if you need anything else today, call. I'll check with the tribe and find out what may have happened today at the reservation."

George looked at Lightfoot and said, "All right, I'll see you tomorrow then. It's been a long day."

Lightfoot walked back down the street with George. They split at Lightfoot's car. Lightfoot waved as he drove away.

George headed out to see Gus, heading toward Swede Road just a mile north and parallel with the road where Chief and Rowena lived. He would start there and return to stop at his cousin Pete's house on the way back through.

It appeared to George that Gus was headed out to the barn to do chores and then turned to see who drove into the yard. He recognized George and smiled. "What brings you out here, Sheriff?"

"I'd like to talk for a minute, if you have the time."

"Sure, I have a few minutes. What's on your mind?"

"I understand you and Pete were at the bar last Tuesday night?"

"Yes, we were, but we only had one and left. Went in to warm up after fishing. You know we aren't the drinking kind. It was a rare occasion. Pete and his wife had an argument, truth is we didn't fish. He wanted to discuss it with me."

"While you were there, did you overhear anything unusual that was said?"

"Like what?"

George waited for it to sink in.

"We did hear loud excited voices, so loud we had to leave to continue talking. I needed to help Pete work out his personal issues with his wife, so we went back to my home and finished our conversation. He drove home from there. They made up, and everything is back to normal."

"So, Pete will say the same thing?"

Pete stepped out from the cow barn and said, "I sure will. I'm sorry, but I couldn't help but overhear the conversation. I didn't want to interrupt until you were finished. The wife and I are fine now."

George looked amused. "Okay, if you two remember anything about that night, please come in and talk with me."

They both nodded as George turned and left.

CHAPTER ELEVEN

Jeffery Beacom, the Schnicklefritz

George went back to the office, cleared his desk, and locked the evidence and notes made by Lightfoot in the top drawer.

Just as George was leaving his office, Jeffery Beacom entered. He was a medium-framed man with a squirrelly demeanor. He wore a felt hat with a tiny red feather in the headband, a pair of jeans with a green flannel plaid shirt, red suspenders, a butterscotch-colored unbuttoned jacket, a pair of high-top leather boots that were a bit too big, which caused the toes to turn up, and a pair of gray wool hunting socks with a red stripe at the top where the stuffed-in jeans caused them to bulge.

"Good evenin', Sheriff George. I couldn't help seein' the twins visiting you ta'day. Any reason?"

"That was yesterday, Jeffery."

"You're right, it was."

"Just visiting, Jeffery," George responded. "The usual, talked about Two Shoes."

"I supposed that was part of your conversa-shun, I been wantin' ta talk to ya 'bout somethin' I saw."

"What's that, Jeffery?" George straightened in his chair.

"Ya know, I heard Two Shoes tellin' Stubby about the money in Peabody's safe Tuesday night. I couldn't help hearin' what he said. He sure was talkin' loud. I think everyone in the bar that night heard him. He was excited, I could tell by the way he was tellin' about it, an' he had a few beers before he began talkin'. Pierre heard it, he was sittin' the closest. Even the bartender heard. She tried to catch our attention by telling jokes, like the one about the two boys standin' in front of the grocery store with their bib overalls and straw hat, chewin' a timothy hay stalk, the one said to the other one, 'Have you been farmin' long?' Wal, they all heard Two Shoes, nevertheless."

Jeffery "had the floor," while George listened to him. He looked like a Schnicklefritz, jumping all over while he chattered away. George related Jeffery's actions to his Schnicklefritz that hung on the wall of his bedroom. His mother gave it to him when he was young; he had it ever since. It was made in Germany, a wooden man with moving joints and a pull string. When the string was pulled, it would raise its arms and legs in a precarious way. This was exactly what George thought of when he saw Jeffery with his big grin and jittery mannerisms.

Ironically, just at that time, Jeffery raised both arms, bent at the elbows, and continued, "Wal, the next night, I'm tellin' ya, I'm walkin' east along the road to De Tour Village, an' I see a tall fig-ure with a dark hooded jacket. Walkin' fast too, he was. An' all of a sudden, the wind caught somethin' from his grip and carried pages all the way across Bay Street, flyin' here and there. I ducked in the shadows until that figure passed. Why, he didn't even try to get what blew away. I scooted across an' began pickin' these pieces of paper up. Why, I thought I'd never get them all picked up before they blew all the way to Moran, or even Escanaba." Jeffery had his arm pointing straight west. "I looked at them under the streetlight on the corner, an' they looked like they might be valu'ble, they's 'bout eight or nine of 'em, so I took that stone the twins use to keep the door of the hardware store open in the summer an' placed them in the entrance up against the door, weighed 'em down with that big stone. They'd know what to do with 'em."

"You aren't giving me some malarkey, are you, Jeffery?" It was all George could do to keep from laughter, although it could be a lead, and a good one at that.

"I swear, sure as I'm standin' here." He slapped his knee with his right hand.

"It was eerie. I could hear music, and it came a floating through the wind. It scared me, sure."

"Tell me more about the figure."

"Tall, taller'n me."

"That wouldn't take much, Jeffery. You're only five-foot-two with boot heels on."

"Well, I'm tellin' ya that's true, but he was tall."

"How many people have you told this to?"

"No one, I swear."

"You don't say."

"No, an' he had somethin' else to do. T'was like he wanted to throw away those papers. I don't know why, but I saved them."

"Did you go back the next day to see if they were still there?"

"Nope, I figured the twins, they'd know what to do with them."

"Did you keep any of them?" George looked up from taking notes. "If you did, you should turn them into me."

"George, it's hard not to tell you da truth." He reached into the inside pocket of his jacket and pulled one out and handed it to George. "I kinda wanted it as a keepsake."

George reached over the desk to take a closer look at it. A pungent musky odor came from it. He held the bond closer to his nose to be very sure the bond was what he smelled.

George quickly took notes while he tried not to let Jeffery know how excited he was about this news, if it was true. Jeffery had a history of making up things just for attention. This bond convinced George that there was some truth in Jeffery's story. Pondering on that, he realized a few things about Jeffery. He was a nervous fellow, never sat still, and he also reminded George of a leprechaun from Ireland; he even wore red suspenders. He had one eye half shut, and the other bulged open, looking hard over the inkwell, papers, tablets, mugs, and books on the desk to the pad where George wrote.

"Did ya get 'er all, Sheriff?" He jammed his hands in his pockets. "I guess that's all I have fer now. Guess I'll be leavin'."

"Well, I'm glad you came in, Jeffery. Thank you. You've helped me a lot." George was standing. "If you think of anything you may have left out, let me know. Remember, don't repeat any of this to anyone, I mean *anyone*."

"Got it!"

Jeffery was out the office door and through the front entrance within seconds.

George began to turn out the lights when he felt a presence and turned to see Marie Sutherland, who stood in his doorway. She wore an aqua wool sweater and gray slacks. The collar of her white blouse lay over the neck of the sweater, dividing the blue of the sweater, which complemented her blue eyes. She smiled at George. Her naturally curly, honey reddish long hair hung to her waist and framed her face.

"Looks like you had a very long day, George. Leaving now?"

"It's about time. A lot happened today, and I really am hungry."

"What's on the schedule for tomorrow?"

"More of the same. You know I can't tell you details yet."

She was at the door ready to leave. "I know. Its' okay with me. Just be careful. When it comes to murder, people's personalities change."

CHAPTER TWELVE

A Break from Routine

George followed Marie out and locked the main entrance door. Looking at the cute little way Marie swung her behind, George checked himself and thought, *I'd better keep my mind on the good meal my wife has cooked and go home.*

He started his truck and turned east towards his home and his sweet wife.

George could smell the roast pork and scalloped potatoes as he entered and then saw the freshly baked apple pie she made. He followed the aroma to where it sat on the counter, cooling.

Nutmeg and cinnamon drifted under his nose. "Hey, what smells so good?"

Isabel turned from the sink, smiling. "Your favorite, George, and pie to boot."

"Makes a man want to come home every night."

"The oven warms the house after a long cold winter day."

"It sure does. You sure are a special lady, Isabel."

"Thanks, George." He reached for her and gave her a big hug. Things led to a detour before eating.

They were almost finished with the meal when the phone rang.

"Yes, it's Isabel," she answered. "You want to talk to your brother?"

"Just a second. Here, honey"—she handed the phone to George—"your brother, Fredrick, needs you for something." Isabel began to clean up the kitchen area.

"Hi, Fredrick, what's up?"

"One of the cows is trying to give birth, and she can't do it alone. I need your strength, along with mine, to pull when she has a pain. She's down with her tongue hanging out, and I'm worried I may lose her."

"I'll be right there."

George looked at his wife and knew right away she was upset by the expression on her face.

"Do you want to ride with me? It shouldn't take long."

"No, I need my rest for work tomorrow. I know you are needed, but when will you be home with me? This happens all the time. I'm just tired of it all."

George turned and left. *Our marriage needs renewing, Lord, and we need your help. I truly love Isabel. She is beautiful, a hard worker, and the very best cook ever. I'm gone so much, yet it is my job. What should I do, Lord?*

George drove in silence north and east to the farm area near the quarry. It took just ten minutes driving to the 320-acre farm. Fredrick came to meet George as he drove up.

"Glad you got here so fast. Dad insisted he could do this, but since his heart attack, I don't want him to try."

"You're right, it won't take long, and we'll be finished."

Fredrick had looped a length of binder twine around the calf's two front feet, handed it to George, and grabbed a hold of the twine too.

"She's ready, pull!"

The little nose came through and started to squeeze back into its mom's body. "Hang on." They both pulled as hard as possible, and the cow started to push again. "Pull, pull."

First came the nose, head, and then body, followed by the tail and hind feet, and it slid out onto the barn floor. Mama cow turned around and began to lick her newborn, cleaning up the calf. When it was cleaned all over his body, the mama cow nudged it to get up.

The tiny legs shook and wobbled until he could hold his ground and weakly stand.

"Maa." It wobbled and fell and then struggled to get on all fours again. Nature took its course, and the newborn calf began to bunt his mom, looking for a dinner of milk, sucking out loud, and smacking away to what seemed to relieve the mother cow.

The brothers laughed.

Fredrick and George waited to make sure the cow would pass the afterbirth. Many a time the cow would need help, so they waited. An hour later, they walked towards the farmhouse, relieved to know all was well.

Hot chocolate and cookies greeted them when they came in the back door. Mom Kaughman waited at the kitchen table with an apron over her long-sleeved flannel nightgown, her hair pulled back and braided in one long train that hung down her back, and a tired smile on her face.

"Well, what do we have out there? Are you tired? Dad went to bed."

"No, I didn't." Their father stood in the doorway of the kitchen with a grin on his face. "Had to see how things went in the barn."

"Come sit down, Dad. The calf is here, and the cow is fine. It's a heifer. We'll go out a little later to see how she is," Fredrick said.

"A heifer, such good news. Oh, George, Isabel called. She sounded upset. She wondered when you would be back. That was over an hour ago. I'm sorry, George, I didn't want to tell you, but I felt it was necessary because she may be angry if I didn't tell you," Mrs. Kaughman said.

"That's all right, I'll sit a while to warm up and then head out."

George sat in the overstuffed chair and fell asleep almost immediately. His mother quietly laid a quilt over him. She went to the phone and called Isabel to let her know.

The sun on George's face woke him the next morning at seven fifteen; he looked around and then remembered he was at the farm.

I need to get home. Isabel will have left for work at the school, but if I hurry, I will have time to clean up before Lightfoot meets me at the office.

"Morning, Mom, got to go. Did you hear from Fredrick this morning? I wonder how the cow is."

"Stop down to the barn as you leave. Fredrick's out there now."

"Thanks, Mom. I'll see you Sunday morning in church. Will you be at the funeral?"

"Yes, we'll be there, son. Let me know when it will be."

"Let's see, today is Thursday. The fourth day is Saturday. After four days, the fire keeper will have sent smoke to the Great Spirit, *Gitchi Manitoo*, preparing his spirit for its journey."

"Yes, George, I spoke to Rowena about what I could bring for the feast."

"Good, you are so thoughtful, Mom," she said as he went out the door. "See you Saturday."

George quickly walked down to the barn. Fredrick had the milking almost done.

"Morning. How's the cow and calf?"

Fredrick stood holding a twelve-quart bucketful of milk. "Both are fine. Thanks for coming to help. It seems so good to know you are only a few miles away and that you are willing to come when I need you," Fredrick said.

"Brother, I'll always be here for you, Mom and Dad. I was gone to college for four years when I was young, but I don't foresee my leaving for any given length of time from now on. I know that was hard for you at first. You were younger then, still in high school, and had to do the chores before you left. Getting up early is the hardest."

"It was at first, but now after ten years or so, I'm used to it." Fredrick laughed as he sobered. "You know, George, I never told you this, but I resented the fact that you went off to college and found a job other than helping Dad and I here on the farm, but now I realize you weren't trying to shirk your duty. The farm income is good, but it wouldn't be enough for you and Beatrice at that time." Fredrick paused. "I'm sorry, George. It was a terrible thing, how she tried to have the baby, and…but who knows? Maybe someday I may find a nice woman and marry too."

"I'm surprised you felt that way, and I appreciate your being candid. I could say this is the most you have talked to me in a long time."

"It's because I really worried the cow and calf would die. She was on her last thread of energy when you came immediately. You lost your best friend just a couple days ago, trying to adjust to your loss, investigating, and taking time out to help me." Fredrick hugged his brother. "I'm sorry for you that your best friend is gone. It's good you have Isabel."

"True, it is. Thanks, and now I have to get back to meet Robert Lightfoot to continue with the investigation. There are a few pieces to the puzzle that has started to fit together. When this is done, I will probably have it solved."

Fredrick took George's hand and began to shake it when George reached and hugged him again.

George became nostalgic as he backed out of the farm driveway; many memories remained on the farm, and they were good. One day in winter, George decided to learn to ice skate. He donned his skates at the edge of a flooded muck hole and stood up. Sliding and slipping, he was almost to the middle when he fell and broke through the ice. The water wasn't deep, but George was wet through the behind, nevertheless. The hard part of this lesson was to have his brother and parents see his wet clothing and his hurt pride.

He recalled memories of their childhood, the time Fredrick was learning to milk cows. He did fine on the first two cattle, but the third one was a young heifer, first time milked. She rolled her eyes at Fredrick, raised one of her hind legs, and kicked him in the face. That was a close call; it left a scar on his cheek. Then came the long harvest days when they shocked the wheat and waited for the threshing machine to get to their farm. All the farmers in that area took turns helping others get the harvest done. During harvest, his mom made dinner for all of them, including four pies for desert if they had the room for it.

One time, he was learning to drive the old John Deere. He would drive the wagon to load the shocked grain. He jerked the clutch out too fast, knocking the neighbor off the back end of the wagon. The neighbor picked himself off the ground and grinned from ear to ear.

———————

Lightfoot arrived at the office just as George drove up. Maria was across in the news office busily typing at her desk. George glanced to the right through the beveled glass windows that divided the two offices. She waved and kept clacking away on the typewriter as she was completing an article for the *Breeze* paper. George admired her for the challenge as she followed her father in the news business. Earlier in her life, she was a tomboy and grew up following her father, Mr. Sutherland, until she learned everything about the writing and printing press from him. Many times he had thought to put curtains or Venetian blinds for privacy, but George enjoyed the company of her presence.

"We've lots to do today, right?" Lightfoot asked.

"Morning to you too. Hey, I forgot to tell you, Lightfoot. I did talk to Jeffery Beacom. He wandered in my office right after you left last night. He had a story that has me questioning the truth of it, yet it does open my mind with more questions."

"Really, what did he tell you?"

"Long story short, he said he saw someone the night of the robbery. Some papers flew out of that person's grip, the wind skittered them every which way across Bay Street. He continued by saying he gathered them and piled them in front of the hardware store then weighed them down with a rock." George added, "You know how the entrance door is recessed with the two showcase windows on each side? This protected the papers from blowing away. I guess the rock was heavy enough to hold them down, even though it was so windy that night."

"And the person didn't try to grab them?"

"Apparently not, according to Jeffery, the man in the black hooded jacket walked swiftly in the direction to where he was going."

"You need to talk to the twins again, eh?"

"We need to, yes. And Peabody," George said.

"Well, let's go!"

They each raised their coffee cups and finished them. George rinsed the cups in the tiny sink in the lavatory. Lightfoot had slipped into his insulated vest while George was gone and waited at the door. His premature white hair made his smooth bronze complexion stand out, complementing his appearance. The two strolled across to the hardware store.

The morning sun made a glare on the store windows, reflecting across Cedarville Bay.

As he entered the store, it appeared there were no apparent customers in the hardware store at the time, so George began, "Good morning, boys, are we alone?"

"No one but the two of us," Wilber said.

"I have been told about more evidence, and I hope you will tell me instead of my having to ask."

Wilber took a long look at Gilbert and then nodded in affirmation.

"Thursday morning, the morning after the robbery, when we arrived at work, there was a gift sitting at our door. We weren't aware there was a robbery at the time."

"Go on."

"Come, let's sit down in the office. We can see if anyone enters from there." Gilbert led them to the back, where his enclosed office was windowed to see incoming customers. Lightfoot noticed that Wilber was rubbing his hands nervously.

Once they were seated, Gilbert said, "There was a rock, our rock that we use to prop the door open. Under the rock early Thursday, just a slight dust of drifted snow covered the rock, but under the rock were the papers, noticeable because they curled at the corners, bringing a normally larger circle of snow that raised around the stone."

Wilber continued in his usual, almost apologetic whine. "We thought it was a gift at the time."

"That's true," Gilbert said. "Now we realize it is quite a coincidence to get a gift the morning after a robbery. Since no one asked about them, we thought we were in the clear."

"You could be, as far as I know. Peabody only had money in his safe. However, I'm disappointed that you didn't tell me prior to today. It makes me unsure of your honesty, even though they showed up on your door step and you didn't steal them."

"We're sorry we didn't add this to your first inquiry, George, and if you want the money back, we can work something out," Gilbert said. Wilber nodded his head in affirmation.

"As far as I'm concerned, at this point, they were not a part of the robbery. Thanks for coming clean on this issue. Let's keep this under your hat for the time being."

Gilbert and Wilbert stood side by side with a wide grin on their faces. "Thanks, George. It really was a godsend. We are so broke."

George and Lightfoot nodded and strode back to the sheriff's office. When they were out of earshot, Lightfoot began, "Tell me about Bearer Bonds. I don't know much about them."

George looked at Lightfoot and answered, "The fact is they are good for anyone who holds them like a signed check. Anyone can cash them. I believe the twins have already cashed them. Truth is, I do not care. They need the money worse than anyone here in town. But if there were bonds in Peabody's safe, and these are the ones that the boy's thought was a gift, we have a different situation to clarify."

"You're right, they do need the money, according to their testament, but it makes me wonder why Peabody didn't tell you about them, if they were his."

"I believe he has the answer to that question, and I will try to get it out of him as soon as he returns from work at the school."

George looked at Lightfoot and asked, "You'll be with me, won't you?"

"I will."

"How 'bout us going across to the bar and getting some of that good stew Bonnie makes?"

They had stood in the sun talking until their decision to cross over. "I think that's a good idea. We can't see Peabody until all the students are gone, and he finalizes things in his office, say around four in the afternoon."

As they headed across, Lightfoot glanced across in the direction of his tribal car, which remained where he parked it near the news office.

It was another mild January thawing day. Water trickled off the roof, which made George duck as he went into the bar. Lightfoot found a table in the corner where their voices couldn't be overheard. George joined him, and Bonnie followed.

"How can I help you today?"

"I'm going to have a bowl of that stew Sally made with two slices of her homemade bread," Lightfoot said.

"Ditto," said George. "And lots of butter."

"And a pitcher of beer and two glasses."

"That's right, we can think better after a couple glasses, eh?" George asked Lightfoot. They both grinned.

George had found a new friend in Robert Lightfoot. At first, he wasn't completely relaxed with him. After a few days of working together, a bond began to build between them. Lightfoot was Two Shoes' cousin. There were similar gestures and expressions Lightfoot made like his buddy, although Lightfoot was slightly taller than Two Shoes.

"Bonnie, when you get a break, can you come over here for a couple minutes?"

"Sure, you bet, I'll be right back," Bonnie replied.

"Going to ask her about the fishermen?" Lightfoot asked.

"That, and anything else her pretty little face can tell us." George winked at Lightfoot, and they both laughed. Each knew what the other was thinking; once she got started, she couldn't be stopped.

Bonnie joined the two men as soon as she cleaned up the cooking area. No one was in the bar except George, Lightfoot, and herself. She drew up her chair and asked, "Now what is on your mind, George?"

"I was wondering about the two men you were telling us about, one was called Sam?"

"That's right."

"Did you recall anything that they talked about? Or where they were staying?"

"They were looking for something besides fish. They stayed at Smith's Landing, I remember them talking about that."

"What do you think they were looking for?"

"Well, they said they were road builders, and I think they were speculating. I think they were checking out the roads here, they do blacktopping. I believe they were in hopes they could get the contract to do it."

"It's not a bad idea, but that would give outsiders the work we need here in our area. You said they stayed at Smith's?" George asked.

Lightfoot leaned closer and said, "That opens a new can of worms. They were there all along. They could have seen who did the dastardly deed, or one of them may have done Two Shoes in, but why?"

"Smith must have their addresses. We'll go over to see him when time allows."

"Sure, Smith would." Bonnie looked excited.

"Anything else about these two that you can recall?" Lightfoot asked.

"They are married but don't wear wedding rings. I overheard them talking about their wives. They came on to me, but I didn't give them the time of day," Bonnie proudly said.

George cleared his throat and said, "I mean something that has to do with the robbery and murder."

Bonnie blushed, giggled, and said, "Sorry, I guess I wasn't thinking."

"That's all right, Bonnie, we understand. It does tell us something about these two, even if it isn't directly related," Lightfoot said.

They finished and left her a healthy tip. Once out of hearing, George said, "Let's go over to Smith's and have a talk with him." The two headed back to where the sheriff truck was parked.

"I'll ride with you," Lightfoot said as they reached George's truck. He slipped into the passenger's side of George's truck.

"Funny Smith kept this from us before, but maybe he didn't take the opportunity to. Or didn't think we needed to know."

"Ya, he can give us the address of those guys. Who knows what they may be able to tell us."

George parked the truck at the edge of the grass in front of Smith's Landing. The snow had melted enough to reveal the intricately designed red brick walkway to the front door.

The building was built with stone and wood. Small as it was, it was attractive and well built. The entrance revealed a long bar with a beveled glass mirror along the wall behind it. Below the mirror was a carved red oak shelf that housed various amounts of liquor bottles. The bar stools were upholstered red, which matched the oil cloth tablecloths on the two tables to the right or left. The office was to the left through a solid oak door, and a stone fireplace decked the wall to the right as well as hall leading you to the kitchen. A moose head decorated the wall above the fireplace opposite a twelve-point buck near the office door.

They seated themselves on a stool at the bar. A fire crackled in the fireplace.

"Be right out," Smith called from the back. They could hear the woodstove door slam shut, and smell the wood smoke roll into the front room where they waited for Smith. He came out drying his hands on a bar towel. "Is this social? Can I give you a drink or duty?"

"All three."

Laughing, he asked, "What will you have?"

"Budweiser."

"I'll have one of them too."

Smith set the bottles up on the bar and placed glasses beside them. "What are you, guys, up to today? Have you solved the crime yet?" He partially filled each glass.

"Two Shoes. That's why we're here. We have a couple questions you may be able to answer. You had two guys here last week from down state renting one of your cabins, right?" Lightfoot asked.

Smith looked surprised at Lightfoot and answered, "Yes, they left and went back home. Why?" Smith asked.

"Well, we need their names and addresses and their phone numbers, if you have them."

"Wait a minute, let's be clear on which two guys you are asking about."

"The two guys that stayed here from Lower Michigan came here to fish but was never seen out on the ice, or were they? Seems like you'd know that, Smith."

"Is there a reason that…?"

"They were in the Cedarville Bar the night Two Shoes was last seen."

"Okay, yam, sure, just a minute, George. I'll get them from the office records." While Smith went into the office, George drank his beer and refilled the glass.

"Here they are, I wrote each one down. But why do you need the information?"

"Maybe no reason, just routine. We need to question everyone who was in the bar Tuesday evening," Lightfoot said.

George added, "This leads to a question I need to ask you, Smith. Did you see anyone talking to Two Shoes this past week? Or see anything out of the normal?"

Smith looked from George to Lightfoot and back. "I can't think of anything. As far as I know, the guys never did go out to fish. They said it was too cold."

"Can you remember where you were last Tuesday night? And did you see Two Shoes anywhere since last Tuesday?"

"Last Tuesday night, I was right here, George. As for Two Shoes, he hasn't been here fishing all this week. Except I do recall seeing him, well, he was here Friday afternoon for a while, but I thought he went home, and then I helped you on Saturday morning."

"Did you see anyone else out there besides Stubby?"

"Nah, nothing, except now that I think of it, I was just returning from town when I pulled into the drive, and I noticed a guy wearing a dark hooded jacket. He walked swiftly away from my yard towards town. I never thought any more about it."

"Describe him."

"Tall, slim, walked away, couldn't see his face with that hood."

"How tall? As tall as Stubby, like he is over six feet tall?" George asked.

"You don't think Stubby...? Not as tall as Stubby." Smith scratched his head. A frown raised on Smith's forehead. "This guy could have come from my place or just walked down the road away from the point towards town."

"You can't blame me for asking because someone here in this small community is a murderer," George said. "There have been two crimes committed this last week, and I mean to find the one or two people who did them."

"I hope you do. This has left me with the jitters."

"Everyone who saw anything is at risk, and if the one who did the crime wonders what is said, he could come and do harm to anyone who has offered the truth about it. You should have the jitters, Smith. Be careful and cautious. We need to solve this murder as soon as possible to protect our people from further danger."

"I won't tell anyone what we said today."

"Keep your doors locked and be careful. Get as much information from your visitors as possible." George looked at the piece of paper with the two fishermen and added, "Checking to see if you added phone numbers, Smith, thanks. With the help of Lightfoot, we will solve this crime quickly and thoroughly." George folded the paper and put it in his pocket. "Remember, keep your doors locked and don't trust anyone."

CHAPTER THIRTEEN

A Peabody Tale

Lightfoot left for home. He had tribal responsibilities to fulfill. It was his responsibility to keep law and order among the tribal residences in the immediate area, which included the entire Bear Clan that reached west from halfway to St. Ignace, east to Detour, and north to midpoint, which was called at this time the Donaldson area. The reservation was a small limited area near the water just west of Hessel, but the Osagwin chief was given a plot of eighty acres north where the Dixie Highway headed west. The lumber people needed the land to transport the logs from the water to their destination. Some of the tribe stayed, but almost all moved to the eighty-acre plot. Others bought land and built elsewhere.

Lightfoot was single, so he also had the responsibilities of his home and surrounding land that included snow removal in winter and yard and garden in summer. He would be busy checking Two Shoes trap lines for, at least, another week; at that time, Chief would have made a decision what he would do about them. George knew this and looked gratefully at Lightfoot's back as he walked toward his car. He had been a great help in two ways, investigate with George, and help George reclaim his life after Two Shoes.

George looked at his gold pocket timepiece, which was chained to his belt; there was ample time for him to talk to Peabody before Isabel would be home and dinner ready.

George went into his office and wrote down the events of the day. He and Lightfoot visited Smith, Bonnie, and the Shepherd twins, and he also related the information that Jeffery told him. He had shared all that Jeffery Beacom told him to Lightfoot earlier that day. That finished his update in the journal.

Five minutes later, George sat down the ink pen and dialed Peabody. George spoke into his phone. "I'd like to come over, I have a few questions for you and Tilde. Is she home?"

"Sure, what is it about?"

"Well, Peabody, it can wait until I get there. Some new evidence has come up I wish to share with you."

"All right, we are home now if you need to come right away."

"Yes, in fact, this is a very good time."

George had finished his work at the office. He put away everything that was a part of the murder investigation, turned out the hallway lights, and locked the front beveled glass door.

During the short three-and-a-half-block drive north and east to Peabody's home, George pondered about how he would bring the subject of the contents of the safe. The content was the big thing. Peabody had told George he didn't want Tilde to know about how much money there was in the safe. Whether this was true or not, he would respect Peabody and question him separately from his wife. After he finished talking to Peabody, George would talk to her.

Peabody answered the door, "Come in." He gestured to the office to the right.

George could see the slender body of Tilde standing in the kitchen, hair pulled back in a bun, busy cooking or cleaning up. He stepped into Peabody's office.

Peabody closed the door. "Have a seat," he said as he seated himself behind his large mahogany desk.

"I have the results of the prints taken from your homestead, and none of them match anyone from the files except yours and Tilde's."

"This doesn't sound helpful for your investigation."

"There were partial prints, but none were enough to match nor none that are registered."

"What were you needing from me today? Do you have something more to ask or tell me? New evidence, you said?"

George looked towards the bedroom. "Can I look one more time in your bedroom?"

Peabody had a puzzled look on his face. "Sure, right this way."

George noticed the safe door was still open, not all the way but still ajar. He stepped closer to check out his hunch. Sniffing near the opening on the safe, he smelled the same musky scent that was on the bearer bonds. "Have you moved anything since I was here last, Peabody?"

"No, what is this all about?" Peabody asked.

"There is a witness that puts evidence that may couple with your robbery. However, I need to ask you again, did you have anything in your safe beyond the money you reported to me?"

"What kind of evidence?"

"What else did you have in your safe?" George bluntly asked.

"Come back in my office, please, George." Peabody gestured in that direction. George obliged; he knew this was tell-it-all time. He closed the door behind him and sat down.

Peabody looked agitated, his eyes sparking into near rage, and he hung his head for a moment and then said in a low voice, "There were some bearer bonds and an onyx statue."

"Onyx statue. Why would you keep an onyx statue in a safe? Was it very valuable?"

"Not so loud, I didn't want Tilde to know I had them." His shoulders rounded and hung, while his whole body seemed to sag.

"Do you want to share this? Is there an explanation for all this secrecy?" George said softly.

"Tilde and I have been together for a long time, forty years to be exact. We were married even before we graduated from college. She had to leave school and go to work. Her parents stopped giving an allowance after we married. They thought it would be better if we both graduated first before we married, but being young, we went against their wishes and were married quietly in Lansing near the college.

"We kept trying for a child to no avail. Eventually, we began to drift apart. She went to card games once a week, and I remained busy with my job. Then one summer day, I met a lady at the ice cream parlor. She invited me to sit with her at the little round table in front of the shop. I had a chocolate sundae, and she was eating a strawberry sundae. I can remember it like it was yesterday. She had dark auburn hair, shoulder-length, and she was built like the girl in the Coca Cola advertisement. You know, the one with her holding the bottle, smiling, and wearing a yellow bathing suit. Alice was wearing a one-piece yellow bathing suit and covered it with a white beach robe. She was built like a million. She had curves and breasts that made a man look twice when she was around. Tilde, well, she always was very slim." Peabody leaned back against the swivel desk chair for a moment in thought.

To him at that moment, George was not there. "We walked down to the beach, talked about everything and nothing. We just needed each other's company like a dry sponge needs water. She spent summers on Marquette Island. During the school year, she taught geology at Michigan State University. We would collect rocks during our walks. Before long, we became lovers. Our trips were secretly hidden from everyone. At least, I have never been approached about what I was doing. I was in love." He paused.

"She was in love too. We escaped one day and went to Mackinaw Island for the afternoon and evening. She came from a wealthy family that had purchased a small log cabin on Marquette Island back in the twenties. She called it small, but it was a mansion. The cabin had eight bedrooms with a bathroom between them and three floors. The maids stayed in the attic level. There was a grand piano in the L-shaped living room with a grand view of Hessel Bay to the north. Alice had the cabin to herself, as the family rarely came north, perhaps an extended weekend. It wasn't hard to take my fishing boat and skirt around the islands, pick her up, and be on our way for a wonderful afternoon. We took her cabin cruiser to the island that day."

"Okay, let's tie this in with your safe."

"Well, like I was telling you, we were in love, and one day, Alice gave me an onyx statue of a black bear she had purchased in Mexico.

She wanted me to have something to remind me of her while she was gone in the summer. I couldn't put it out where Tilde would see it, so I put it in the safe. I could have, but I didn't want to address the questions, where I got it, why, and most of all, I didn't want to lie to Tilde or destroy the compassion the onyx bear held for me. From time to time, I would get it out when Tilde was gone playing cards. Just touching it made me feel as though I was near Alice. We had two wonderful summers together."

"What else did you have in the safe?"

"I already told you, just bearer bonds and the statue. Alice gave the bonds to me. She said we would have money to run off with. That was our dream. Then I heard she had an accident and that she would never walk again." Peabody began to sob. "She broke it off, saying she would never come back to Marquette Island again. The bonds and the onyx statue were the only objects I had to remember her by, and now they are gone too." He wiped his eyes with his white handkerchief. He turned away from George to hide his tears.

After a moment, Peabody said, "Memories." His voice cracked. "Just memories are all I have."

George could feel his pain and loss, yet he had to go on with the investigation. He reached over and patted his shoulder and gently asked, "Peabody, just one more question. Did Alice wear a musk perfume?"

"Why do you ask?"

"Because the safe has a musky odor, possibly from old papers or her perfume. Possibly from…"

"Don't. It hurts so bad to think of her. Yes, the bonds did have a faint semblance of her perfume."

"Peabody, this is a very unfortunate story you have portrayed to me. I can't ask any more, nor will I have to talk to Tilde. She will not hear anything from me about your treasures. Three of the five-thousand-dollar bonds did show up. How many did you have?"

Peabody heaved a big sigh and said, "There were ten altogether. George, I'm hoping you will get the bonds back, and I do hope you solve this crime and retrieve my money."

"Peabody, do you realize the value of the bonds alone was magnitude? What were you thinking? I can't guarantee their return, unless the thief has them in their possession when he is arrested. However, the three that was found will be returned to you or the money amount. I can't promise that I will get all the money or all the bonds, but I guarantee you I will search until I have caught the perpetrator. Whatever I can secure of the robbery will be returned to you. It will only take the right clue or one slipup by the perpetrator to complete my inspection. Lightfoot and I will continue until we find the robber and the murderer. I promise I will not give up until I have found the person."

CHAPTER FOURTEEN

The Two Fishermen

The smell of roast beef reached George the second he stepped out of his truck. Isabel smiled at George and said, "Welcome home, I just finished dinner."

"Hey, it smells like roast beef and the trimmings."

"Beef roast with carrots, potatoes, peas, celery, and biscuits in the oven." Isabel pointed at the Home Comfort cook range.

George grabbed Isabel at the waist and twirled her around.

"Put me down, George, or you will not get fed anytime soon."

———————

A good meal and a full night's rest were all George needed to start the next morning fresh and ready to continue his search for the guilty culprit.

He entered his office and noticed that Marie wasn't in the news office yet. The lights on the west side of the building were not on. George began the day by calling the first man on the list that Smith gave him. *Sam Wainwright from Harbor Springs, hmm, not that far away*, George thought.

Cranking the phone for Stella, he waited. Finally, the answer came. "Stella, can you connect me to Harbor Springs, five-five-five, please?" A few moments later, he said, "Hello, this is Sheriff Kaughman from Cedarville. I would like to talk to you about something that happened last week while you were here on vacation."

"Oh, what would that be about, Sheriff?"

"I was told you and your friend was in the Cedarville Bar last Tuesday evening. Did you hear or see anything out of order?"

"Well, I don't recall anything."

"So you're saying that you didn't hear anyone talking about money that night? Tuesday night, you and your buddy were in the bar, right?"

"I did hear something but not all of it."

"Did you stay in a cabin on Les Cheneaux Channel? You know, The Snows Channel?"

"We did rent a cabin, but I'm not remembering what the name of the water was."

"Well, did you rent from old man Smith at Smith Landing?"

"Yes, that's where we stayed."

"And you didn't see anything out of the ordinary out on the ice any of the days you were staying there."

"I only saw that tall guy and the Indian fishing through a hole. They were there almost every morning. I couldn't understand how they could stay out there in that kind of weather. It was so cold, unbearably cold."

"You say they fished out of one hole?"

"Oh no, they each had one of their own."

"And you say they were there every morning?"

"Well, I take that back. They were there the first two days and then again on Friday."

"What days are you talking about? When did you come up here?"

"I'm thinking we arrived on Sunday morning and didn't see them until the next morning, so I guess it was Monday and Tuesday."

"What mode of transportation did you take, boat or airplane?"

"We flew into Kincheloe, rented a car, and drove down here."

"I see, and you didn't see anything else or see anyone else out there at any given time?"

"Just once, Smith walked over to the edge of the ice and looked out over the channel, that's it. It's none of my business if I did, so I didn't see anything."

"Well, Sam, I'll be talking to you again. Thank you for your straightforward honesty."

"You are welcome, good-bye."

Lightfoot walked in while George was talking to Sam Wainwright. He sat back in his chair waiting for George to complete his call.

"So he didn't see anything?"

"No. I can guess he knows more than he admits. I'm going to call his buddy now."

George waited while Stella connected him. His name written down by Smith was Joe Knapp, who was from Indian River.

"Hello, Joe?" George asked. "This is the sheriff from the Les Cheneaux area. I want to talk to you about something that happened while you were up here last week. Do you have a moment?"

"Sure. What's this about?"

"I understand you and your partner, Sam Wainwright, was here for a week, stayed at Smith's Landing, and possibly was at Cedarville Bar last Tuesday night. Is this true?"

"Yah."

"Well, one of my friends was in there, and he was talking very loud about something he saw. Did you remember what he said?"

"Yah. That Indian was talking about all that money he saw, and I think everyone in the place heard it."

"So, you and Sam heard it too?" George began to dislike Joe Knapp's attitude. *At least, he admitted he overheard Two Shoes talking last Tuesday night.*

"Give an Indian a few drinks, and they go crazy. Ya, we both heard it, that's what I just told you."

"Let's go back a few words," George said with emphasis. "Two Shoes was a Native American, *Anishnaabi*; 'the first people.'"

"Ya, I noticed you two were close."

"Yes, we were very close friends almost all our lives."

"Too bad he's dead."

"How do you know this?"

"Smith told us the morning after you took him out of the water and placed him in the coroner's wagon. We went in to settle the bill before we left."

"Well, Joe, did you hear or see anything from Friday noon to dusk that may help us find the murderer?"

"Not me, I didn't see anything, except that guy who was walking towards town right before dark."

"Was it Stubby, Two Shoes' fishing friend?"

"I don't think so. This guy was a little shorter, like my height, but not as fat as me." George looked at the phone with a puzzled look.

"How tall are you, Joe?"

"Five-foot-ten inches," Joe replied.

"Do you remember anything more about that guy? What he was wearing or how he walked, like did he have a limp or anything else that was notable?"

"He wore a dark hooded jacket. He walked fast and didn't look either way."

"Did you ever talk to Two Shoes?"

"Not me, I only saw him in the bar and from my window at the cabin while he was fishing."

"Joe, think, did you see Two Shoes after Tuesday night in the bar?"

"I never saw him again until Saturday morning when you two pulled him out of the water and ice."

"How did you know it was Two Shoes?"

"I really didn't know. I assumed it was since I didn't think anyone else would be at that fishing location."

"I'm surprised you and Sam didn't come out to help us. You know, curiosity and all."

"We were packing and getting ready to leave. We didn't want to butt in on you."

"Well, I appreciate your respect for the crime scene, the criminal investigation, and procedures. If you think of anything else, let me know. Lightfoot and I are investigating this together. Robert Lightfoot is the 'res cop,' 'white men' call him the High Sheriff."

"Okay, I will remember that. Give me your phone number."

"It's four-eight-four."

"Thanks."

George made a mental note that Joe didn't respond or ask why anyone would kill this man. After he hung up, George shared Joe's side of the conversation with Lightfoot.

"Funny," Lightfoot said. "He saw Two Shoes when he was there, not the same thing that Sam saw. They were both together, but their stories don't correlate."

"I figure Sam was not telling everything he knew."

"One thing I didn't ask Joe was if Sam saw the man in the hooded jacket," George said.

"You'll probably have the opportunity to do just that when you are working the final facts together. I have a feeling you will have more questions for this guy."

The phone rang while they talked. "This is Joe, I do remember one thing Friday night, almost dark. The wind blew in gusts. There was a man walking across the yard and towards town. Does this help?"

"Can you describe him, Joe?"

"What I remember is that he walked with a deliberate pace and wore a dark hooded jacket and jeans."

"Anything else?"

"That's it."

George hung up, looked at Lightfoot, and said, "Ironic, he remembered the guy with the hooded jacket, he called it. It's true, things are becoming clearer as we go on with this."

"Here comes Jeffery Beacom, wonder what he has on his mind." Lightfoot stood up when he entered.

"Hello, Jeffery, come on in and take a seat," George stated.

Jeffery took off his hat and sat on one of the straight chairs against the wall, pulling himself closer to the desk. "I just 'membered somethin'. That night, I saw the papers flyin' in the breeze, wal, that guy was a comin' from the direction of Peabody's house. An' then I 'membered somethin' else. Peabody has a girlfrien'. I saw them mor'n once. An' he's not the only one, but I can't tell who the other one is."

"Then why did you bring it up?"

"Well, well, I forgot. I promised not to tell."

"All right, Jeffery, I guess the secret is out. But you had better not spread any malicious gossip. Mum is the word." George made a sign like he was zipping his lip shut.

"Jeffery, how long ago did you see Peabody and his girlfriend?"

"Last summer."

"Have you seen her since then?"

"Just once before it snowed, this past fall."

"What does she look like?"

"Dark red hair, blue eyes, and a figure like ooh-la-la."

Was she in good physical condition?"

"Like she was running to get into the car?"

"Where was that?"

"At the schoolhouse."

"Have you seen her since last fall?"

"No, not since then."

"Thank you, Jeffery. If you think of anything else, let us know." George nodded at Lightfoot.

"I will," Jeffery said, looking straight at George and ignoring the "us."

After the front door closed, Lightfoot said, "That little beggar doesn't like the thought of me helping with the investigation."

"It's not that, Lightfoot. He is just ignorant and doesn't respect or know Native Americans' values and customs."

"I'm glad that you are different. I noticed Pierre Bouchard acted the same as Jeffery. Pierre sure didn't want to talk to me that day we were out on the trapline, and he was upset when you told him that I would do Two Shoes' traplines until further notice."

"Hmm. What Jeffery told us makes me think that Alice came back to see Peabody last fall."

"I wonder if there is any truth in what Jeffery said." Lightfoot mused.

"What I'm wondering is why Peabody didn't tell us he saw Alice last fall," George added.

CHAPTER FIFTEEN

The First Day of the Viewing

After Lightfoot left, George sat at his desk looking at notes taken of the murder. They began the day that Two Shoes was discovered in the ice. The journal had the time and how he was taken to St. Ignace for the autopsy. The conversations with Stubby and Mr. Smith were briefly recorded. The next entry was the following Monday, after Drake and the coroner, Zimmerman, from Williamston, Michigan, co-examined Two Shoes' body. There were also details of their findings, along with their decision that it was homicide. He and Lightfoot had gone out to talk to Pierre Bouchard.

George stopped reading and leaned back in his chair. "I think Bouchard was telling the truth, even though I believe he was poaching Two Shoes' traps." George leaned forward, placing the chair flat on the floor, and returned to his journal. He noticed how he had talked to the Sheppard twins. Their finding the bonds helped them get out of the financial troubles, but now he would have to get them to pay Peabody back. The twins had work-related alibis that night. *I wonder*, he thought, *if I could still help by returning the three bonds and have the twins make arrangements to repay for the "two" they found. The remaining could still be in the hands of the thief.*

Looking down the list, he noticed where he had talked to Bonnie and the two fishermen, Sam and Joe. Yes, and Bonnie, Pierre,

Smith, almost everyone who was there that night when Two Shoes was last seen.

George stood up and looked out the window. He could see the corner where Meridian Road headed north out of town. George was thinking again about the two fishermen. Sam and Joe had something more than fishing on their minds. They were road builders. Possibly they wanted to get the contracts to blacktop the road north to Sault Ste. Marie and west over to St. Ignace via highway the Dixie Highway. That could keep them in work for at least two or three seasons.

George was pacing back and forth while deep in thought about the two fishermen. If they weren't honest about what they saw, it could possibly affect their chances of doing business here. *And because they don't want to jeopardize a foot-in-the-door opportunity for the jobs, I believe they were being honest with me and Lightfoot,* he thought.

He returned to the list on his desk and read the next entry. The next couple entries were Gilbert and Wilbert Sheppard and finally Peabody again.

"There has to be something I have overlooked, some simple clue. What?" George ran his fingers through his thick blond hair. He reached for the phone and had Stella ring up Lightfoot. Lightfoot answered almost immediately.

"Lightfoot? I have gone over all the notes you have jotted down, researched everything I have recorded. I'm in a dilemma. This is the first murder case in all of my twelve years since I worked as a sheriff. Regardless of the fact that the murdered person was my best friend, I'm at my wit's end. I've had stabbings over arguments between two drunks, I easily arrested the men on the spot. Another case was the hit-and-run. I found the guy, arrested him, and he went in for manslaughter. It was easy too, witnesses had his license plate number and description of the car. Not a problem to find him within a few days. This one, Lightfoot, is different. Somewhere I'm overlooking the facts. Am I putting my personal feelings in the way?"

"Well, would be understandable, even if you were. Keep plugging at it, sooner or later it will jump up right out of nowhere, and bingo! George, you need a break, go home, get a good meal, rest, and get a long night's rest. You'll feel better in the morning, believe me. I've been there, and it works. You will get a fresh view in the morning."

"Thanks, pal, I needed to hear that."

George stood up, pushed his chair under the desk, turned off the lights, and locked up for the night.

On the way home, George walked past the hardware store. The rock sat snuggled in the corner of the entrance to the hardware. *If it could only talk*, George thought.

Isabel had dinner ready for him when he arrived home. George noticed a huge pot of vegetable barley beef soup on the stove.

"I'll have supper on the table right away. I made some soup for the tribe. I thought I'd better make something since there have been so many people already coming to talk remembrances of Two Shoes and tell other stories."

"I smelled the soup, thought it was our supper."

"No, I made chicken, potatoes, and peas. It's in the oven keeping warm."

George went into the bathroom to clean up for supper. When he came out, he said, "Isabel, have I ever told you the customary way of the first people, Anishnaabek?"

"I can't recall if you did, George. What is it?"

First of all, two elders are given tobacco and asked to do the ritual. In this case, it was Chief. He asked Lightfoot and John, you know, the elder who leads the pow wow ceremonies."

"Oh, yes, I remember John."

"The family will gather the cedar and boil it. Then they will drain the cedar water in order to do a purification bath before the embalmment."

Isabel listened intently as George continued, "Lightfoot and John went yesterday to do this. They will bring the body back to the great hall as soon as the undertaker completes the embalming. I expect they brought him back last night."

"Thank you, George, for telling me this. I never have been to a Native American funeral before. What do they customarily do next?"

"Now that he has been cleansed and embalmed, he will be viewed for four days."

"I heard he was there at the hall. My friend, Jeanette, and other folks were talking at school about it. When I came home, I made the soup for tomorrow. Maybe we can take it over tonight yet because I don't have room in our small refrigerator for it."

"Hey, will we eat first?" George said, thinking rest will come soon, but this is important to her.

"Okay, but can we take the soup over yet tonight?"

"Sure. Let's return thanks and eat, and then we'll go."

Fifteen minutes later, they were in the truck headed to the tribal center. When they arrived, they saw many cars outside the main building. Smoke sifted out of the top of the lodge where the fire keeper remained, feeding the fire. Isabel looked at the lodge, which prompted George to tell her, "The smoke will rise to make the path for his journey."

Isabel went to say something in response when George interceded, "Remember, Isabel, his name should not be spoken until after the four days and the funeral because it will interfere with his journey."

"Thank you, George. I needed to know that."

George carried the large soup kettle, while Isabel went ahead to open the door to the main building. The large room expanded from the south where a fireplace burned with the flames dancing warmth to visitors. A clock hung above, ticking time. To the right, Two Shoes lay in the casket with flowers around him. There was a long davenport and two overstuffed chairs. Some wooden folding chairs were placed between to afford extra space for more visitors. The kitchen was behind the large room to the left where there was a large pass-through window with a stainless steel counter to place food. The door to the kitchen was just to the left of the center of the large community room. The large room had three rows of long tables with wooden folding chairs for those who were eating or just resting and visiting.

Men were dressed in their very best attire; some had blue jeans and plaid flannel shirts. Some wore suspenders to hold up their pants, while others used a leather belt. The women wore colorful skirts flowing to the floor, while the cooks wore their hair piled high in the fashion of the forties resembling the Andrew sisters with sweaters belted around their waist.

All looked their way as Isabel and George entered. Some whispered to each other, but most knew George. They knew how much he cared for his friend and showed him the greatest respect. John and Henry came forward to meet him and Isabel as they entered. Sally, a large woman with her hair braided in one long braid wound around her head with pins to hold it in place, took the kettle of soup from George. She wore a gingham dress with a full apron that covered her front from her neck to her knees. Her homemade buckskin moccasins were worn for comfort while she cooked and arranged food for the visitors.

"Thank you, George. We can truly use this."

"You'll have to thank my wife Isabel," George said, pointing to Isabel.

"Thank you, Isabel. We appreciate what you did to show your kindness at this time," Sally said.

Isabel smiled and turned towards George, who had headed over to the casket area.

Sally shuffled back into the kitchen. You could hear her singing lowly to herself.

The north third of the great room held the casket. George's friend was surrounded with bouquets of flowers and overstuffed furniture. The casket was made of pine. John, Henry, and Bob, the three elders, built the casket and had it ready the day before. Lightfoot took it with him when they did the purification bath. The undertaker put Two Shoes into the homemade casket for his ride back to the tribal center.

George stepped in that direction. Two Shoes looked as though he was sleeping. He was covered with a star quilt made of many colors. His aunt and her quilting group had made this for just such an occasion to show how much their community loved him. Reaching into his pocket, George laid a fishhook that Two Shoes made into the casket. Other items were already there—a dream catcher, his war medals, an eagle feather and more. On one side, a long braid, salt-and-pepper in color, was tucked under his arm and through one hand. It had belonged to Chief, his father.

Isabel joined him, and they both stood looking at Two Shoes for a few minutes. Isabel reached over and placed her arm around George's waist. He took her hand, and they walked away towards the door.

On the way home, Isabel stated, "This is so new to me. I have never had close contact to a wonderful tradition as this is. We were there for just a short while, yet I could feel a difference in the ways of Two Shoes' people."

"Yes, I really like the traditions of this nation," George said.

"I noticed the smoke coming out of the very top of the lodge. Will you go in there?"

"Eventually, I will. The fire keeper has lit the fire and will keep it burning for four days."

"And all the time people come to pay respects?"

"Yes, and they pray to the Great Spirit. They bring things of remembrance to put in Two Shoes' casket with him. Many will sit with him and tell the stories they remember about him and what they did together."

"Will you do this?"

"Yes, but not until..." He paused and swallowed. "Not until the last day."

CHAPTER SIXTEEN

The Second Day

The second day of Two Shoes' showing began early for George. He woke and stretched wide to loosen his bones. It was a good sleep. He was truly rested.

Normally, Isabel fixed breakfast for her husband, George, but today she left for work before George was awake. George found a note on the kitchen table. It read:

> George,
>
> *I have made another pot of soup for the tribe. It is on the back porch keeping cool.*
>
> *Please take it over to the community hall today.*
>
> *Isabel*

Of course, he would deliver the pot of soup. He planned to attend each day of the traditional tribal funeral functions. First, he wanted to take this time to have closure with Two Shoes. Secondly, he needed to get acquainted with those who loved Two Shoes and shared the same feelings and times with him as he himself had. Third, George felt he would find clues from those who attended each day. One of them was the murderer. Of this he was sure, and in time, something would come up to show him the way to the truth, how it happened, and why it happened. Ironically, most murderers like to return to the crime scene or be with those who are sharing their loss.

He made a bowl of oatmeal, some toast, and a cup of coffee. He liked the toast spread with real butter all the way to the edge, making it good to the last bite. It had to be whole wheat, and the oatmeal would have brown sugar and real cow milk, which he brought from the family farm once a week. After breakfast, he shaved, washed up, polished his boots, and put on his dress uniform. He took the pot of soup from the back porch, placed it on the passenger's side floor, and left for the reservation. *I should have washed the truck*, he thought. But that would be difficult with the cold weather. He had plans to be professional and alert yet wear a smile when necessary and listen for most of the day.

When he arrived at the community hall, there were a few people sitting around the casket, talking in low voices. George recognized most of the men there. Gordon, one of the helpers, looked his way and said, "Hi, George, come over here."

George lifted the pot up and said, "Be right there." It was good to see people he knew. He was unsure at first. The Native Americans mistrusted the white man, even though he was very close with Two Shoes and his family.

George went to the kitchen with the soup where he could smell the fry bread and the roast in the oven, which floated out into the great room. The ladies were in the kitchen preparing the food, including Sally who perspired, showing little beads of perspiration on her forehead and upper lip. She had pulled her hair up into a bun. Iris, a tall, slim woman who looked about fifty-five years old, stood peeling potatoes. She blushed when George looked her way. The third woman, Rose, was short and plump. She busied herself rolling out pie dough. A kerchief was wrapped around her head to keep her hair back. Normally, she was seen wearing a pill box hat, which she usually wore to church and when she went to town to shop. Today she wore a white blouse overlapping the waist of her long aqua-colored skirt.

George nodded at her, and she smiled.

"That's Rose, she is shy," Sally said as she took the soup away from him. "Thank you, George."

"Isabel sent it. It's corn soup. What smells so good?" George asked.

"It's the venison. First, we marinated the meat with herbs and garlic. It was kept in the refrigerator for two days, thawing and marinating. Earlier this morning, we placed the roast into a large roaster, added more spices and salt and pepper, and placed it in the oven," Sally explained.

"My, does it have a mouthwatering odor. I'm full, but I could eat more."

"You stay away from the food, George Kaughman. It isn't ready yet," Sally said as she laughingly scolded him. "One o'clock is soon enough."

"Okay, I'll stick around just so I can have some," George said.

Any fear of being accepted faded after the great conversations with the women while they cooked. George left the kitchen with a slight smile on his face. He ambled over to the group sitting near the casket, seated himself quietly, and listened to the men talk.

"The one time we were out hunting"—Gordon, the older man who wore lots of turquoise jewelry around his neck and wrist, was talking—"he was there with my cousin, Bob, Joe, the fire keeper at that time, and me. We were sitting quietly in a huddle, waiting for something to come along to shoot at. Along came a rabbit, and Joe whispered, 'Too small.' We waited in silence for a long time before we heard a snapping of branches and grunting sounds. We all looked at the same time to see one of the biggest bears we had ever seen. 'I'll get him,' he called to us as he ran straight towards the bear. 'You're getting kind of close,' Bob yelled. 'If I get too close, I'll beat him to death with my gun stock,' he called back to us again."

One of the listeners from Arizona asked, "Did he get the bear?"

"Of course, he did. He ran with him for at least a mile before he got the bear so tired that he only had to wait for the bear to stop for a rest, and then he shot him."

They all laughed.

"It is a good story," the man, who sat in the overstuffed chair near George, said.

"We really missed him when he went into the Army," another man, who was leaning against the support column, said. "He was gone for over two years. The Great Spirit was watching over him those days while he fought for our country. We didn't expect to see him return. So many were killed at Normandy, but lo and behold, he walked back into our lives with that same grin he always had on his face as though it was yesterday that he had left."

Thoughtfully, one man said, "He had changed some, a little quieter, but he still wore that great smile." They nodded in agreement.

Two men sat together on folding chairs wearing full dress regalia. A headdress of eagle feathers donned their head, bone breastplate, with feathers and silver conches over their beige colored long sleeved shirt, and leather chaps over their jeans adorned with conches and beads through leather strips hanging along the outside seam. Their feet were covered with knee-high moccasins with beaded designs on top and leather fringes along the outside seam.

Their complexion was dark from exposure to the sun, with deep wrinkles, and their dark brown eyes were sunken in. They appeared to be much older and were possibly from the west. They looked at George with curiosity. Perhaps they didn't know why he was there and how he cared for him like a brother. George held their gaze until they looked away and began talking among themselves again. George made a mental note to ask Lightfoot about the two old men.

Chief was sitting on the davenport, talking to his cousin, John, who was telling stories. A man whom George had seen quite often at the pow wow sat beside one of the drummers and talked about the many times they had gathered wood and fished together.

"The year he wanted to build a canoe was a good memory," Frank, the drummer, said.

"Yes, I remember. The three of us, you, me, and him, walked a long time in the forest looking for a birch tree the right size and age. Finally, we spotted one and began the toil of cutting the precise depth to not kill the tree but thick enough for ample coverage on the frame of the canoe," Gordon said.

"He couldn't wait to get his hands busy peeling. After peeling off the birch bark, he carried it out of the forest to the truck box. He wanted to ride in the truck box with it to the garage where we made the frame," Frank added. "Then when we told him we needed the rosin from the tree to seal any cracks to keep it from leaking, he was anxious to go right now to gather the rosin."

"We told him another day," Gordon said. "Then he asked, 'Why not today?'"

"We went out for near a week to gather enough rosin for one canoe. He wasn't even twenty years old then. He learned that year how hard it is to make a canoe and do a good job."

The group chuckled together and enjoyed another good story. George smiled to himself. He could remember how much he missed his friend while he built the canoe, but he was helping his father and brother with planting on the farm at that time.

George looked at the clock on the wall above the fireplace. It was eleven thirty. The door of the community hall opened, and Lightfoot entered dressed in his hunting garments, lined buckskin pants and jacket with a hooded Alpaca jacket over that, and fur-lined knee-high moccasins. He had just finished running Two Shoes' trapline, the one closest to the community hall and on out towards Pine River. George stood up to greet him.

George shook his hand and said, "How was the trapping?"

"Chief will be happy to hear there were two coyotes, one fox, four beaver, and several muskrats, around eleven or twelve."

"Good news."

"Anything new here?"

"If you mean leads on the murder, not yet." George lowered his voice when he answered, and then he added louder, "What do you think of the food cooking?"

"Makes a man hungry. When will it be ready?"

"Sally said it would be around noon."

"I'm headed to clean up and be back for dinner."

George followed Lightfoot outside, walking with him for a way towards Lightfoot's cabin out behind the hall. They stopped when they reached the cliff. Looking below, they saw the vast cedar swamp with birch, poplar, and cedar trees at first and then beyond low bush huckleberries and more cedar and pines. Farther back, they saw Pierre Bouchard tracking along the trapline. It was far enough away that Bouchard didn't see or hear the men above.

"What do you make of this guy?"

"Hard to say, he is a strange one," George said.

"When I first looked, I thought it was my cousin in the distance. Shaking my head, I had to know it wasn't him," Lightfoot said.

"It's because you have seen him so many times out there." George raised his hand, gesturing in the trapline direction. "At least three times a week. I guess it would be natural to think it was him."

"Or his spirit," Lightfoot said.

George stood looking down, thinking for a minute about seeing the "spirit" of his best friend; he changed the subject by saying, "This cliff is quite a drop, isn't it?"

"Oh, possibly fifty feet down, and then the cedar swamp begins. Up here it's sand and gravel." Lightfoot stood for a minute and then said, "I'd better get on and clean up. See you back in the hall."

George nodded and watched as Lightfoot headed across south to his cabin. He noticed the snow was melting again, and Bouchard was getting closer to the hall. Bouchard didn't look George's way. George noticed the snow was only up to Bouchard's ankle before he turned towards the hall. The January thaws would end soon, and more snow would return in a few days.

While Lightfoot and George were outdoors, the tables were set up and ready for dinner. Some of the neighbors and family began filtering into the hall. Primarily, they went to say a few words to the departed and to his relatives and friends. The postmaster from Cedarville entered, viewed the casket, placed a small trinket in the casket, nodded to George, and sat with his friend, Howard. Jim and Geraldine Smith came in from Pickford. Smith shook George's hand and said, "How are you holding up?"

"Doing it," George answered with a wry smile. Mr. and Mrs. Smith went over to the casket to view Two Shoes.

George stayed where he was, waiting for Lightfoot. Chief also joined him.

"Have you seen the pelts Lightfoot gathered today, Chief?" George asked him.

"Not yet, but I heard it was a good day."

"Is Rowena here today?"

"Yes, she is in the kitchen helping with the meal. We'll save a seat for her and Lightfoot," Chief said. An additional special place setting was beside Rowena's in honor of the departed one.

Sally, Iris, and Rose were setting up a buffet along the wall near the kitchen. The soup and bowls were at the end and then came the venison, potatoes, corn soup, beans, corn bread, fry bread and six pies, berry, cherry, apple, rhubarb, pumpkin, and custard. Coffee was set up at the end with cups, sugar, and cream.

A prayer was sent up to the Great Spirit, Gitchi Manadoo.

Then anyone who wanted a meal went up to the buffet, filled their plates, and sat randomly throughout the hall. The *wasichu*, white man, mixed with the others and began eating.

Lightfoot entered the hall with his tribal sheriff uniform, badge, and holstered gun. He walked up to George and said, "Ready to eat? After that trap run this morning, I am famished."

"Let's go then. Come on, Chief, please join us," George said.

"Go ahead, I'm waiting for Rowena. We'll be there soon."

George looked in Rowena's direction and noticed a beautiful bouffant hairdo, sculpted up and pinned with several decorative combs. She wore a dress suit of a dark navy blue color and two-inch heels. He looked in approval.

"There are many *jhaginaash*, white eyes, here today," said one of the men from Arizona.

His brother-in-law nodded and answered by saying, "He was liked by many. It shows by the respect they have for him."

George overheard them, which reminded him to ask Lightfoot who they were.

"They are distant cousins from northern Arizona. They married into the Hopi clan there and heard about their cousin. It was only natural for them to travel that far for such a situation as this. Older, they are suspicious of all, especially the jhaginaash."

Lightfoot and George filled their plates with everything available on the food line. They had to return for the coffee and a piece of pie.

Just as George was sitting down to eat, the front door opened, and Bouchard entered his dirty leather buckskin jacket, leather leggings, and boots. His hat was in his hand, and he hesitated to come in closer. Bouchard looked in the direction of the casket, stepped over in that direction, and looked down at Two Shoes, his trapping enemy lying still in his final sleep. No one said anything to Bouchard. George began eating, not looking in Bouchard's direction. George glanced at Lightfoot and the others at his table. They ate and acted as though Bouchard was not there.

Bouchard took off his buckskin jacket and laid it on a chair near the casket. He placed his hat on the jacket and strolled over to the buffet table. Taking a fork and plate, he took venison, fry bread, and a cup of coffee and walked over to the farthest end of an empty table. As he sat eating, the elders came to him one at a time.

"You are here to show your respect to our loved one?"

"Yah," Bouchard said and bit off another chunk of venison, chewing with his mouth open.

"Did you know him well?"

"Nah." Bouchard kept eating and never looked up.

John's eyebrows went up and then back down.

"The tribe and I are pleased you came to show your respects. He was liked and loved by many."

"Yah," Bouchard said.

"Have anything you want. There is pie too, six kinds. Goes good with coffee," said Gordon, another elder who had joined John near Bouchard.

"Thank you, I didn't rob his traps or steal his pelts. He was a good man."

"Thank you."

John and Gordon offered to shake Bouchard's hand. Pierre rubbed his greasy hand on his leather chaps and shook hands with them.

"I guess he's made friends with two major people in the tribe," Lightfoot said to George. "As loud as he talked to them, Bouchard got around to telling us the answer to the question we have wondered for some time."

"I still think Bouchard got a share of his pelts," George said. "When there is a hunch, it usually is the truth."

"For his sake, it is better if he hadn't," Lightfoot said.

Chief looked at Bouchard and then to his friends, George and Lightfoot, and said, "I wasn't aware that my son didn't trust Bouchard. I'm sorry I was listening in on your conversation."

"You might as well know what is going on. That's why I've been checking his traplines. I'll keep doing it until you have someone else you prefer to do it," Lightfoot said.

George explained, "Chief, I asked Lightfoot to do them for you. You have enough on your heart right now. We will take care of your business of the traplines and anything else you need done for now. Please let me or Lightfoot know if there is something you need, and we will do the best we can to get it done for you," George said.

"Thank you for your help. Right now, all I'm thinking is getting someone to dig the spot where we will place the casket in the ground. It is at the Italian cemetery up on the hill on Dixie Highway. Our section has a wooden sign with 'Ojibwa' carved into it. I'm sure you've seen it, George," Chief said.

"Oh yes, but this is the first time I'll be going to the Italian cemetery." He hesitated for a moment. "My first wife and baby son are buried in Pickford at Cottle Cemetery east of town. Now my best friend will be buried out here west of the reservation in two days. My guess is the thing you want most from me is for me to find your son's killer," George said.

Just then, the door opened, and a man in a wheelchair and a younger woman entered. She pushed him through the door and looked around the room. The man spotted the casket and pointed towards it. She pushed him in that direction. John and Chief were right on their heels and talked to the two strangers. "Hello," John said to the man and woman.

"Bamapii, hello. I was with him in the war. He saved my life."

"Welcome. Are you hungry?" John and Chief both pointed to the buffet.

"Not right now. I want to set here and remember to you the things he did and to share them with you. He looked at Chief and said, "You're his father, aren't you?"

"Yes, I am, and his mother is sitting right over there with the fancy hairdo and navy suit."

"Yes, she is beautiful. This is my daughter, Sarah, and my name is Jerald Hodgekiss. We live in Engadine, drove over this morning, and it took longer than we expected it would."

Chief said, "Come and eat, you can share with us after we have finished."

"Thank you, I guess we are hungry. Are you, Sarah?"

"Yes, Dad, I can eat something."

She helped her father set up to the table, went over, and filled his plate, brought it, and went back for a plate for herself. When she returned and sat down, George and Lightfoot introduced themselves to the two.

"We were just finished when you came in the door. Can I get some pie for you?"

"Sure, anything as long as its berry," Sarah said.

"You are wondering where my wife is, she passed away while I was overseas." He looked down for a moment and then continued, "But I have the sweetest daughter. She has been so good to me. You know, it seems as though I know you both because he always talked about you."

Chief and Rowena were pleased to hear this. They nodded and smiled.

Later they went back to the casket. Many followed, wanting to hear why this man was here with his daughter and how he knew Chief's son. The two from Arizona sat to his left, John, Lightfoot, and George also sat close. Chief and Rowena sat to the right of him. A group of near thirty were gathered. They waited silently to hear him begin.

"He called me Jerry. We were in the same platoon, he was the careful one, always thinking things out first, and I volunteered for everything. There was a cave that needed investigating. The sergeant saw action going in and out of the cave, but finally it seemed they were gone, or they were dead. The sergeant said we needed the cave, so I volunteered to go in and check it out. I did wait at the opening first to see if I could hear anything for a long time. I couldn't throw a hand grenade in because the cave may collapse, so I stepped in carefully and inched my way along the wall, stopping to adjust my eyes to the dark. Suddenly, from nowhere, I heard shots going off, and I fell to the ground, bleeding like a stuck hog from several places. I took my gun and shot in the direction that the firing came from. I heard a cry of anguish and a thud. I lay there bleeding and wondering where my radio was. I felt around me on the rough base of the cave and finally touched it. I tried to call out, but it was no good. A stray shot destroyed it. I knew I needed to stop the bleeding. I tried to get up, but both legs were useless. My left arm was hanging worthless as well. I began to feel weak and passed out. When I woke, I was being carried lifeless across someone's back. I passed out again. I woke again when I fell to the ground. We were under fire from the enemy. It was dark when we finally could move on. Once again, I was being carried safely through enemy territory and finally back to our company."

"Three days passed before I was seeing, hearing, and feeling better. I looked at the chair next to my bed, and it was him sitting there with a grin on his face. He saved my life. I'll never forget it."

"It took a long time to heal, and they shipped me home just before the war ended. I was no use to the war without two legs and half an arm. But I can say he saved me, and he is a man who deserves great honor. I would have died in that cave if it wasn't for him."

All the men made cries in favor of his bravery. Some slapped him on the back. His daughter, Sarah, smiled at their reaction.

"Stay until after. We will have a celebration in his honor."

"Yes, please stay. We have room." Chief coaxed Jerry.

"Thank you, but we must return. I wanted to see him one more time. I have, I will never forget him. Now we must go."

Sarah helped him put his vest back on and she her coat. They headed to their panel truck where he had a homemade ramp to enter and sit in the front passenger's side. Sarah slid behind the wheel and waved as they drove away.

George returned from the door to where Chief, Lightfoot, and Rowena sat. He reached for his coat and hat, looked back towards the three, opened the door, nodded, and walked out.

He needed time alone. This man's testimony touched his heart deep where he dared not to tread. With a sigh, he headed to his truck.

CHAPTER SEVENTEEN

Friendships Reward

Lightfoot was right behind George and slipped into step with him before he reached his truck.

"There's something on your mind, George, what is it?"

"I need to work it out, Lightfoot. Someone killed him, and for the life of me, I can't figure out why. Why would someone kill him? He didn't deserve to die after being so brave and kind. Have you wondered why?"

"Many thoughts have crossed my mind, but I feel they're best left unsaid," Lightfoot said.

In spite of the snow on the ground, the sunrays felt warm on George's face and back. The sun had lowered in the west, making it near three or four in the afternoon. George looked from the sun through the pines and cedars back to Lightfoot.

"When you're ready, I'm sure you will tell me. Here's what I have asked myself over and over. Did he know more than he told that night in the bar? If it was the robber, why did the robber think he had to murder my friend? After finding out that there was more in the safe along with the money, I began to wonder if the murderer worried that someone would know if he saw the bearer bonds and onyx bear, but how would that be possible? And is that enough to have a reason to kill someone? Unless my departed friend was threatened by saying, 'If you tell, I'll kill you.' But why?"

George's eyes were sunken with a troubled look. The dark rings looked as though he may have not rested as well as he said he did.

"You need a break, George. Take time tonight and get a good long sleep. Sometimes things become clear afterwards."

"That's what you told me last night."

"I was serious. You need to give it a break." Lightfoot suggested.

"I keep going round and round with everything, but it isn't fitting together."

They stood side by side as Lightfoot put his hand on George's back and patted it. "Get some rest, talk to the Great Spirit, and you will get answers. Unless you want to, I can go to the wake for you tomorrow while you get a break. The day of the burial is day after tomorrow. You will be here then, and that's enough."

"We'll see. I'll go into the office and work over the entries in my journal, think out things, and possibly stop out here later in the afternoon."

"Okay, I'll see you then."

Lightfoot waved at him as George backed out of the parking area and onto the road back to Cedarville. Lightfoot stood there in the parking lot until George was out of sight.

George drove on down the hill away from the reservation and out toward Cedarville, mulling over the clues the whole way. As he drove, he prayed for guidance and knowledge. He continued praying until he parked outside his office. He closed by saying, "In your precious name, I ask it."

Across the street at the hardware store, he saw the Sheppard brothers closing up for the night. They waved to him and went out back to their vehicles.

George walked into the office and headed straight to his journal. There may be something here to spark my memory and make way to a new discovery.

"How's it going, George?" Marie asked.

"Hi, Marie, you're still here. I thought you'd be gone for the day. Have you been out to the res hall yet?"

Marie wore a green dress with tiny black and white rings entwining as the pattern. It made her blue eyes look greener. Her hair was drawn up in front with the sides rolled back like one of the Andrews sisters who were singing in the background on Marie's radio. "Don't Sit Under the Apple Tree (with Anyone Else but Me)," the old war song held its popularity. George really enjoyed Marie's company. There was something about her, she was always positive, friendly, neatly dressed, and he felt comfortable when she was near.

"No," said Marie. "I will go Friday, the day of the funeral and burial. I want to cover the story for the news, give my last respects to your friend, talk to the family, and add anything to make a good review for the paper. I know we aren't to speak his name until he makes his journey to the Great Spirit, *Gitchi Manitoo*, so I'll not say his name. I'll probably take a few pictures so I can have a good one for the news article."

"Sounds like you have a plan, Marie. Thank you for your respect."

"And you sound like you're worn out, George. Are you any closer to resolving this case?"

"I'm working on it and have a few more pieces to the puzzle. It won't be long, and I'll have the full picture."

"Is there anything I can do?"

"Thanks, Marie. When I find the answers, I'll have my man. By the way, do you know what Jeffery was talking about when he said he heard music the night of the robbery? Have you ever heard it?"

"He said that?"

"Yes, he said the music came faintly through the cedars and snow. Eerie, it was, and gave him a shiver," George elaborated.

"The only thing I can think is it has been said that old man Bosley, who owned Bosley Island, used to play his violin every night. After he died, the story goes that people could hear music coming from the island and rarely when the winds came from the south. The musical strains could be heard all the way to Cedarville. That could have been what Jeffery thought he heard that night."

"That's possibly what he thought he heard."

"You'll find your man, George. I'll see you tomorrow. I'm going to make a nice roaster of escalloped potatoes with bacon and onion to add to the flavor."

"You, women, you're always thinking about cooking food," George added. "Friday, yes, I'll be there, but Isabel will be working. I'll save a place for you and Lightfoot, if you wish."

"Thanks, George, I appreciate that."

"I may see you tomorrow, but as we were talking, I remembered something. I need to go to Sault Ste. Marie and St. Ignace as well in one day, so chances are small that I'll have much time to check in to the office. Do me a favor, take messages if someone calls or comes in to see me?"

"I'd be glad to, George."

As Marie put her coat on, George helped her into it.

Marie smiled and left.

George looked at his gold pocket watch and realized it was getting late and that Isabel would be home from work.

George remembered the three bearer bonds with the musty perfume smell. He could visualize Jeffery walking here and there, never sitting still for any given time. His hat with the tiny red feather stuck in his hatband and those suspenders. *What a character. Jeffery mumbled forever and didn't come clear about much more that day he came in. He rambled on and on about people having affairs and what did this, and all this rambling have to do with the murder or the robbery?*

George stood up and looked out the front window. Across the way, the hardware store was locked, and the windows were dark. The grocery store was closed as well.

Time to go home. "Talk to the Great Spirit," Lightfoot had said.

CHAPTER EIGHTEEN

Following a Hunch

George unlocked his front door, slid his boots off, and hung his coat and hat on the hooks to his left. He had tucked the mail under his arm and set it on the table and then went in to the bathroom to wash up. Isabel had not come home yet. He wondered where she was. *She probably is working overtime*, he thought.

He picked up the mail and sat in his favorite chair. He reached for the chain to the lampstand and pulled it. The local paper, an electric bill, and a letter for Isabel were all there was. He put her letter back on the table and almost sat back down when he heard Isabel open the door.

"Hey, Isabel, did you work late? I wondered if I should start supper."

"No, I have leftovers. It won't take long to get it ready. What's this?"

Isabel was looking at the letter. She took it into the bedroom and returned within a minute, ready to get supper on the table.

"Who was the letter from?" George asked.

"Hey, Sheriff, is this an inquisition?"

"No, just wondered."

"I'm tired, but I promised to make more corn soup for tomorrow. I'm sorry I can't attend the funeral, but I can't get the day off. Don't forget to tell Sally that Jeanette and I'll come over Saturday morning to help clean up the mess. Everyone who traveled will have left by then, she told me."

"You don't need to make more soup for tomorrow. There will be more people coming to the funeral and burial on Friday. Just skip one day," George added. "I suppose the two men from Arizona will leave early. They will have to fly to Lower Michigan because the ice between Mackinaw straits is still frozen over or get the ice breaker to open the way to go by ferry."

"This is a god-forsaken place to live. You can't go anywhere unless you take a ferry or fly."

Isabel stood at the stove stirring the stew. She turned with two bowls and soup spoons, placed them on the table, poured coffee for both of them, and returned the pot to the stove. She placed a pot-holder on the table and set the steaming soup kettle on the potholder.

George said a prayer of thanks.

Isabel disappeared into the bedroom after the dishes were done. She returned to find George reading the Bible. He set it back on the end table and said, "I had a really long day, and I am very tired."

"Tell me about your day, George."

He took a deep breath and began to tell her everything from early in the morning and concluded by saying he checked the journal for anything he may have missed before.

"What did you do at the hall, George?"

"We talked. I listened to good stories about early years and the things he did with others."

"Who all was there?"

George looked over at his wife. He cleared his throat and began, "There were people from Pickford and two men from Arizona, who later told me they had married women from the Hopi tribe in northern Arizona. They dressed in full regalia."

"What does that mean?"

"They wore a large headdress made of eagle feathers, Conchos, and beaded edges with heavy corded material to hold it together, a breast plate made of bones, Conchos, feathers, and leather buckskin strings. They wore knee-high moccasins with fancy beadwork on the top of their toes and buckskin fringes along the seam. Yes, they were from here. They are cousins to Chief. They really made a picture, Isabel, you should have seen it."

"You are the lucky one. You always can be there and see everything. I have to work. That's all I do is work all the time. I never get to do anything. I'm tired of being left out, not included in anything."

"Isabel, you don't need to work. I can provide for you."

"I need clothes and shoes and fancy things."

"You have shoes, you can't wear more than one pair at a time. You have a Sunday dress for when you go to church with me. Fancy things? You have a nice collection of trinkets now." George said. Then he added, "Isabel, going to the wake, it's part of my work. I had to be there today. It is required, especially if anything should happen. You must accept the fact that my friend was murdered. The murderer could show up. He could cause more trouble. Who knows what could happen?"

"I'm tired, I'm going to bed, you know, I have to go to work by seven in the morning. Oh, and I have to make the corn soup yet."

"Remember I said to wait until tomorrow to make it for the funeral? There's plenty food there now. I'm tired too. Let's go to bed, Isabel."

"I'll come in soon. I need to smoke a cigarette, and then I'll be there."

———————

Temperatures had dropped during the night, leaving George's small cabin chilly when he woke. It was so cold during the night, the windows frosted over, making ping sounds as they adjusted to the lowering temperatures. He stirred the coals in the fire and added kindling and a couple logs, which warmed the area quickly. Isabel fixed breakfast of oatmeal and toast, ate, and left for work.

George cranked the telephone to get the operator. She answered with a half-sleepy voice and connected George to his mother's phone. "Mom, I'm calling to remind you that tomorrow is the funeral. Hope all is well and that you will be able to attend."

"Son, your dad, brother, and I will be there. I know how much you cared for him, and because of our love for you, we will be there."

George cleaned the breakfast table, did the dishes, and took the garbage out to the compost pile. Heading for the garage, he was caught in a big gust of Nordic wind. He decided to go back into the cabin for his heavier fur hat and gloves.

George stopped at the office first before heading to Sault Ste. Marie. He poked his head into the news office and called to Marie, "I'm heading to Sault Ste. Marie. Do you need anything? I can get it while I'm there."

"No, I'm fine. I suppose you will be there tomorrow, won't you?"

"Yes, Marie, I will."

He walked from the hall into his office to get the paper he needed to take with him. His plan for going to Sault Ste. Marie was to check the secondhand, pawn, and jewelry stores to see if anyone came in with an onyx statue of a bear to sell. He started the truck and headed north on the ice and snow-covered road. A few miles of fighting snow drifts and heavy winds brought him to the Rock View corner. There was very little traffic on the snow-drifted gravel road, which made it easier for travel. The cedars and pine trees bent to the wind, shaking the new fallen snow off their branches. At Rock View, he could see the entire valley ahead, including the little town of Pickford. In the horizon, he could see the panoramic view with the tree line and beyond to Canada. Steam flowed from the huge chimney at the Alcoa aluminum plant.

George stopped at Slater's gas station to get gas. He noticed the price was up to fifteen cents a gallon.

"Hi, Luke, sure turned cold overnight," George said to the attendant. "Fill her up."

Luke shoved the nozzle into the neck of the gas tank, locked it on, and began washing the windows. He checked the oil and continued filing the tank. Then he returned to the window and said, "That will be two dollars and fifteen cents."

George handed him a five-dollar bill and asked, "Luke, will you bring back a Hershey candy bar with almonds with the change?"

"Sure, that will be an extra nickel, okay?"

George grinned and nodded.

Luke returned with the candy bar. "Counting back, your change is two dimes, two quarters, and two one dollar bills."

"Thanks, Luke, I'll be on my way."

When George was nearing the old road to Kincheloe AFB, which was located kind of halfway to Sault Ste. Marie, he thought about the two fishermen who were up fishing two weeks ago. Since the war was over, Kincheloe Air force Base was used temporarily for commercial purposes. Word was that it could be opened again for the Air Force if there was a need to.

The fishermen must have flown to the airstrip from downstate and rented a car from the area to use while in the Upper Peninsula or the Mackinaw ice breaker; "Big Chief" could make a trail for car ferries to transport across the straits. He planned to talk again to the two, if he deemed it necessary.

George passed the swamp where he saw a bear last fall. It cantered across the road so fast it didn't even look his way. Passing the Barbeau corners, he stopped at the tiny grocery store for a drink. "Hi, Gracie, have any hot coffee?"

"Sure do, I just perked some on the stove."

"Here's a nickel."

"Keep it, you are doing your job. That's all I need to know and feel safe." She reached for the collapsible aluminum cup George handed her and filled it to the top.

"Thanks, Gracie." He snapped the tin lid over the cup and headed out the door.

Gracie smiled as he left.

By the time his coffee was gone, he was near Sault Ste. Marie. Ralph's Trading Post was down on Portage Street near the St. Mary's River.

Parking his truck in front of the shop, he noticed a few people rushing here and there, fighting the wind.

A bell rang as he walked through the door. The smell of mold and dust hit his nostrils as he entered. "Achoo!"

"Good morning," an old bald man said as he emerged from the dimly lit corner of the room and stood behind the counter.

"That wind off Lake superior sure is brisk today," George said.

"What can I do for you?" Ralph wore a wrinkled shirt with a woolen vest over it and threadbare navy blue slacks. A mole with a long hair coming from it was on his upper lip.

George guessed he was slightly blind because of that long hair. "I'm here to ask you a few questions." George showed him his deputy badge. "Has anyone come in here to pawn an onyx statue in the last two weeks? About eight inches tall, various shades of black, with green glass eyes?"

"Nope, I didn't see one like that."

"Did you see a statue of any kind in the last two weeks?"

"Nope."

George looked straight into his eyes and asked, "A black onyx statue of a cat?"

"I thought you were looking for a beige bear, and I told you. No!"

George reached into his pocket for his card; he handed it to the man and said, "If someone comes in with an onyx bear statue, will you call me at this number?"

The man read the card, holding it near his face, squinting, "Yup, I will."

"Thank you, good day."

He looked a little confused, and George thought it was time the old duffer retired.

He turned the truck around to ascend Ashman Hill, where he looked for the jewelry store. Finally, his eyes caught view of the sign. When he came closer, he saw a sign on the door saying, "Closed until spring."

George knew there was a buy and sell store that sold jewelry halfway back up Ashman Hill on the east side of the street. He would stop there next. Driving slowly, he watched for it. The wind blew gusts of fine snow blocking his view. Finally, his eyes caught the red-lettered sign, "Paul and Lucy's Trading Post. We Buy and Sell Jewelry, Guns, and Musical Instruments."

Again, the wind blew so sharply, and George had to fight his way across the street to the jewelry shop.

A man and a woman stood behind the counter where a glass showcase formed a square horse shoe. On the right of the store, guns of every kind hung from waist high to near the ceiling. Each one looked used and had a neat price tag hanging on a string that was looped through the trigger. The store windows were full of trade-ins. One held musical instruments of every kind, including an old accordion in the original case with pearl trim.

The other window held a collection of various tools and tool and die instruments. In the horseshoe-shaped glass counter were the smaller valuable items—new and used jewelry on one side, the diamonds in front, rings, necklaces, and broaches. A nice collection of various pistols, knives, hunting knives, jackknives, and swords were encased in brass and silver sheaths across from the guns and rifles.

The woman looked at George and then looked at her husband and waited.

George cleared his throat and addressed the man. "I'm Sheriff George Baughman from Cedarville." George showed them his badge and gave him a business card with his identity. "I am wondering if you've had anyone approach you to sell or pawn an onyx statue in the last two weeks."

"As a matter of fact, we did purchase a statue from a very nice man who needed money to get back across the border into Canada."

"May I see it?" George's heart jumped inside his shirt.

"Yes, it's in my safe. I'll get it for you." He turned away towards the back of the store. *He must think it's a very rare piece to lock it in his safe*, George thought.

George walked around and looked at the guns and knives. Only a couple minutes passed when the store owner came out of the back room. George said to Lucy, "Can you give me a description of the man who sold the statue to you?"

"He was tall, had light brown hair, skinny, and wore a tan business coat. The unusual thing about him was that his coat wasn't wool. It was made of a thin material. We considered that he may have come from the South."

Paul approached, saying, "This statue is very rare and expensive. I haven't decided what to do with it yet. Is it the one you were asking about?"

George's heart sank; he was looking at a large jade Buddha statue.

"No, it isn't," George said. "Could you tell me the value of this jade Buddha?"

"It values at three hundred dollars and is very rare."

"I see. I wondered because it is the size of the one I'm looking for. I would like you to let me know if anyone does come in to sell the one I am asking about. It's a bear, black in color, and stands eight to ten inches tall."

"Do you have a number I can call?"

"Yes, it's on the card I gave you. If a lady by the name of Marie answers, it's all right to leave a message. She's the news editor who owns and shares the building with me."

He nodded and said, "I'll call if anything comes up."

"Thank you." George tipped his hat at the woman and began to leave. He turned and asked, "Can you tell me if there is a trader shop in St. Ignace?"

"I'm not sure," the man answered.

"Thank you, I'm headed to St. Ignace now. Thanks again."

George drove south and turned east on Highway 28, which is the main highway to Marquette. When George reached the old Mackinaw Trail, he turned south towards St. Ignace. The winding highway was filled with snowdrifts and wind. Mackinaw Trail pretty much followed the meandering Pine River, crossing it twice before reaching the outskirts of St. Ignace. George inched his way along until he finally reached a landmark of St. Ignace called Castle Rock. The sign read, "Stop and climb, it's still a dime."

A cheese and meat store sat on the left of the road where George decided to get some beef jerky. The jerky would hold him over until he returned for supper. He bought a bottle of Nesbit's orange soda pop, along with the jerky.

"While I'm here, I should buy some extra ground beef and a roast for Isabel."

"How many pounds of ground beef do you want? I have a special six pounds for a dollar."

"Okay, six pounds," George said. Then he and added, "And a four-pound chuck roast."

Hank, the meat cutter, weighed the ground beef and wrapped it in brown meat paper with a string tied around it. He showed George the chuck roast. "How's this look?"

"Just right, a little marbling makes it tender."

Once it was wrapped, Hank rubbed his hands on the bloody white apron and figured out the bill.

George paid the, man and as he was leaving, he turned and asked, "Is the jewelry store still open downtown? Or a trader shop?"

"There's just one on the main strip, you can't miss it. I believe it's the same one you are referring to."

"Thanks."

Munching on the jerky, he headed around a couple curves that followed the water to the center of town near the Arnold ferry line. The combined jewelry and trader shop stood across the street from the bay. George shoved his beef jerky back into the bag, took a swig of orange pop, and wiped his face on a napkin.

By now, George had his talk ready. He walked in and handed his card to the owner.

The store was spacious, holding many gifts for the tourists, jewelry, and the pawned items towards the back. There were original oil paintings along the wall to George's left. The windows had various collectibles of Native American crafts, pottery, leather tobacco bags of various sizes, beaded work, dream catchers, and small replicas of totem poles. The items were elevated at alternate levels, drawing the eye of customers. It was a very nice place where someone could sell for the most money.

"Good afternoon." George pointed to his card and continued, "I'm wondering if you have had someone try to sell you an onyx statue in the last few days. It was a part of a recent robbery."

The man took the card and read it. "Sure, George, what did it look like?"

"Well, the statue is a bear, black marbled in color, and stands about eight to ten inches tall."

"Honey, have you seen anything like what George just described?"

She shook her head. "No, nothing like that, not recently."

George looked closely at her expression to see if she was covering the truth.

"If one should show up, please call me or the county sheriff's office here in town."

"Sure will, George."

Disappointment hit the pit of George's stomach. He turned on his heel and left.

The afternoon turned to dusk. He slowly traveled back the Dixie Highway, heading east to Cedarville. Night was near, and he noticed that Mr. Ambrose was at Thompsons Garage. Probably his truck broke down. George noticed on the right Frank's Groceries. The little grocery store was still open. He stopped to buy a bag of cornmeal. Isabel had said she used the last of her stock. This store sold the best brand of cornmeal in two counties.

"Put a dozen sticks of licorice in a tin bag with the cornmeal, Frank."

"That'll be thirty-seven cents."

George reached into his pocket and paid with the change he got from the gas he bought earlier that day.

"Thanks, Frank. I'll be on my way now."

"Drive careful out there, it sure is storming." Franks voice followed George out the door.

George followed the Dixie Highway and continued east until it reached the Runway Bar, where he would turn south. He noticed the little café was closed, where Two Shoes would eat from time to time when he was checking his western trapline. He liked Millie's Chile.

There it was again, guilt jumped to face him, guilt for not solving who destroyed his friend's life, and disappointment after a whole day of searching and not coming up with one clue.

It was dark when he reached town; he turned south, parked the truck, and went into the Cedarville Bar.

"Hey, Bonnie, bring me a tall one when you get a chance." He took his watch out of his pocket. He had time before Isabel would be home.

"Thanks, Bonnie. How's business?"

"Not bad considering the winter and the snowy night. Tomorrow night it will be full after the funeral."

"True." *Tomorrow is the funeral, and I still haven't any idea who killed Two Shoes*, George thought.

"Bring me a double shot of Jack Daniels, Bonnie." Bonnie suspected he was letting his "hair down" over his troubles.

George drank the beer and swallowed the whiskey in two gulps because he was chilled. He drank down the whiskey and beer quickly and headed out the door.

The wonderful smell of pork met George's nose as he entered the cabin. "Isabel, what smells so good?" George asked, sitting the meat on the counter in the kitchen.

"Don't think you can have any. This is the corn soup for the ceremony dinner tomorrow. I have a new recipe Veronica gave me. What do you have here?"

"It's some meat I got at Tony's meat shop in St. Ignace."

"Did you know Veronica's grandfather is full-blooded Ojibwa?" Isabel said as she placed the meat in a box out on the back porch.

"Oh, I didn't know that. She does have long shoulder-length straight hair, but so do you. What's in the soup?"

"Well, the pork hocks you smell and cabbage, rutabaga, onion, hominy, kidney beans, and chicken bouillon," Isabel answered, wiping her hands on her apron.

"Do you suppose we could taste it since you're cooking it right now at suppertime?" George gave her the little boy look, hoping she couldn't resist his plea.

"I guess there will be enough for us to taste it. Give a hand and help me cut up the vegetables. Go wash your hands first. Chop up the cabbage very small, I will cut the rutabaga and onion. I have to wait for the pork hocks to cool before I can chop them." Isabel handed George a wooden cutting board and a French knife.

"It's awful kind of you to cook these past couple days for the tribe, Isabel. I'm sure they appreciate what you have done."

"I wanted to do something to show them that I do care." She tucked a strand of hair back into her kerchief and continued the food preparation. As Isabel began pealing the rutabaga and onion, she watched George chop up the cabbage.

I wonder if Marie is peeling the potatoes for the scalloped potatoes… oops, I think I had too much to drink, George thought. He grinned but held back a full laugh.

Isabel finished first and dropped the rutabaga and onion into the broth.

"Here's the cabbage. Do you want me to drop it into the pot too?"

"Yes, then you can open the hominy and kidney beans. There's four cans sitting on the shelf. I will be peeling the skin away from the meat and chopping it up to add last."

George went to his thoughts again. *My first wife never used canned beans. She made them from scratch. She was the very best cook. Isabel is Isabel. We've been together for ten years, we've had good times and other times, but it hasn't been all that bad. We need more time to spend together.*

George opened the four cans, leaving them on the counter for Isabel. Then he sat in his chair to read the paper.

"We can't add the beans and hominy for forty-five minutes. I'll put it on simmer and join you."

"Speaking about reading, who was your letter from the other day?" George asked.

"Just someone I knew before I met you."

"I see. What's her name?"

"She's a man."

"Oh? What did he want?"

"He just wondered how I was and if I was still here and working at the school." *A friend from the past? How does he know she works at the school?* he thought.

"Did you answer him? Did you write back?"

"Not yet, but I think it would be polite to respond."

"Maybe, but I am surprised you plan to. I'm not sure how I feel about that."

"I forgot to add the meat to the pot." Isabel went to the kitchen to finish the soup. She went out to take the vegetable peelings to the compost pile and had a smoke before returning.

George dropped the subject, realizing she didn't really want to talk about it.

He read until he became drowsy.

Isabel shook his shoulder. "George, wake up. The soup is ready."

"What? I fell asleep. I'm glad it's ready, I'm hungry."

Isabel had fresh corn bread straight from the oven, steaming hot and buttered. Two bowls of corn soup sat waiting for their supper to begin.

CHAPTER NINETEEN

A Stranger Arrives

In spite of the sun that poked its way through the bedroom window from the east, the weather remained subzero. George heard Isabel building the fire. Sparks snapped, and the door clicked into place with a metallic bang.

He lay for a few moments, remembering a dream that had haunted him all night each time he would wake up. When he fell back to sleep, he would dream it all over again. The vivid distinction that never changed each time was that he dreamed it again, and it would remain in his mind.

He found himself in a huge woods, tall maple and oak trees surrounding him. A deer shot out in front of him followed by three more. Through the mist came a man dressed in a long tan velvet robe trimmed in fox fur. His snow white hair flowed over his shoulders and down his back. He had a white beard and thick eyebrows. He summoned George, beckoning to him to come. George followed the trail, but by the time he reached the place where he had seen the man, he was farther out in the dense woods. George kept trying to catch up to him, but he was always out of reach. The man walked farther away through the haze of the fog until George couldn't see him. When he did, the man looked his way and gestured for him to follow.

George thought, as he lay in bed, about the dream and what it meant. The old man with white hair was a symbol of wisdom, he knew that for sure. Wisdom was encouraging him to remain steadfast with his hunches and follow through until he was satisfied either way.

George shook his head, dismissing the dream, and planted his feet firmly on the cold floor. The day of the funeral would be a long and tedious one, emotional as well as physical.

"George, I put the soup out on the back porch in the ten-quart kettle. I'll have to leave now, or I'll be late. Remember, I'm stripping the floors at the school? Don't forget to remind Sally that Veronica and I will be there around nine tomorrow to help clean up the hall."

George looked out the bedroom door where Isabel stood. She had her woolen coat, babushka, gloves, and a pair of hiking boots on, ready to walk over to the school.

"Do you want a ride? It's really cold out there this morning."

"That's all right, I'm used to it. Five minutes and I'm there." She smiled at him and turned to leave.

When he entered the kitchen, she was out the door and gone.

George went out to the back porch for the soup and brought it in while he prepared for the day. Looking at the lid, he saw a piece of adhesive tape with two words, "Corn Soup," written in number two lead pencil.

George thought that ironically, Isabel loved the back porch. She said this was her piece of home because it was similar to the back porch at home near Flint. The first spring, she planted climbing roses that made shade in the summer as they grew across the lattice board. He walked back in the house, finished eating, cleaned up, and dressed in his uniform complete with the heavy woolen overcoat that was provided as part of his job when he was hired. Today he would really need the warmth while he stood at the graveyard.

Gregory, a volunteer and younger tribal member, stood in the parking lot at the community hall, directing traffic when George arrived. He wiggled his finger, directing George to come over his way.

George rolled down his window, and Gregory said, "I have saved you a spot near the door in case you need to leave in a hurry for another call." He pointed in the direction near the entrance.

"Thanks, Gregory. See you inside?"

"I'll see you later, George, after I get people parked."

George parked his truck and walked into the lodge. He nodded to the *powagin*, fire keeper, where the smudging vessel, a huge abalone shell, sat nearby. The sage smoke smelled fragrant. He offered tobacco, *sema*, smoke, to the Great Spirit, *Gitchi Manitoo*. George carefully remembered not to mention his closest friend's name, as it could keep him from taking his journey.

He stood with the others silently with positive thoughts. George prayed for everything he could think of—happiness throughout the bear clan, prosperity for Chief and Rowena to help fill the void of their loss, and most of all a safe journey for his friend. He left without notice.

He took the soup to Sally, who was in the kitchen with Shy Rose and Iris, who were also shredding cabbage for coleslaw.

"*Aanii*, hello," Sally said to George.

"*Aanii*," George said. He handed the kettle to her.

"*Migwetch*, thank you," she said.

"You're welcome, Sally. The corn soup froze a bit last night. You may want to put it on low for now so it will thaw," George said. He smiled at the other two and headed for the group sitting around the casket. A smudging vessel sat nearby.

A man and his wife from Canada had arrived and were talking to John, the elder who made the homemade pine box.

"You made this casket?" the husband asked John.

Looking straight ahead without expression, he said, "Yes, and my brother helped."

"We have come across the ice to give respect to our cousin and his family. Chief's grandfather and my grandfather were brothers," Sarah Greensleaves said.

"Oh, you have come a long way. I have heard of you. It is good to meet you," John said. "This is the sheriff who is long friends with the family also. George, this couple is from Canada up by Wawa, and they have traveled down and across the ice to be here for the ceremony. They are Henry and Sarah Greensleaves."

George reached out to shake hands with Sarah and Henry. "How was the trip along the way?"

"It went fine until we tried to get across. We went to Sugar Island and then across."

"Try to stay as long as you are here, and I will take time to show you the place where your ancestors grew wild rice."

"Thank you, Sheriff George, but it seems you have a full plate right now. We will return tomorrow morning before the weather changes for the worse. Maybe in the summertime," Henry said, a fearful expression in his eye considering the oncoming weather.

George knew that many of the *anishnaabe*, first people, were leery of the *jhaginaash*, white people. So many of the natives were misused and abused, treated like they were less than human. One story was enough for George to realize how they felt.

George's thoughts roamed back to how the story was told to him. It was told about a young man who came out of the bar and began his drive home. A red light flashed, and the local cop stopped the young man as he began to drive away.

"Crank down your window!" the cop shouted through the slightly open window.

"Why, Officer? I have done nothing wrong."

"I won't hurt you. Get out of the car."

"I'm afraid you will hurt me," he said, but in respect to the officer, he stepped out of the car, anyway. Regardless of his promise, the cop beat him so severely he never recovered. The beating left him crippled. The officer didn't have a justifiable reason for his action, yet it was one good example why *anishnaabe* couldn't trust the white man.

Understanding the Canadian visitor's feeling, he realized someday this would change for the better. George smiled to the couple and said, "I understand. We'll do it the next time you are here visiting." He nodded and went on to the next group of people.

His thoughts changed; this was his opportunity to look around and see if there was anyone suspicious or a stranger possibly acting evasive but nosy. Slowly, he glanced around the room, and someone caught his eye. In the corner, he saw a sneaky-eyed critter that stayed to himself, not talking to anyone. He wore jeans and a blue and white plaid flannel shirt, carrying his overcoat across his arm. His hair was greasy-looking, which indicated it had been a long time from a bath. Spring couldn't come soon enough for him. His boots with a hole on one toe were leather high-tops. Could he have known Two Shoes? Was he a trapper too? He glanced away to another group where he recognized a couple who lived near his folks.

George smiled at the couple from Pickford, who were neighbors to his folks. "Hello, Frank, Hattie, good to have you here. Have you talked to Mom and Dad?"

"Yes, they will be here as soon as possible after the chores and preparation. Your mom has made a wonderful pineapple upside-down cake. I was there yesterday while she was baking it," Hattie said with red cheeks and her hand up to her mouth.

"Just good to see you here, Frank, Hattie." George shook their hands, while John and the others came to join them and welcome the couple.

More entered and went to talk with whoever they knew or were related to. Many from the tribe wore clothing of the style instead of the traditional native attire. The women wore the bouffant hairdos and long skirts to their mid-calf and flared. Pearls were also popular, which she and the others were wearing today. Especially remarkable were the wide brimmed hats, or the pill box with a veil that covered the women's face.

The men, on the other hand, wore their dress suits or ordinary everyday clothing. Some wore a Derby hat.

For two days, the meal was being prepared for families who had traveled from other parts of Michigan as well as Wisconsin, Canada, and as far as Texas and Arizona. The ladies busied themselves in the kitchen in the great hall cooking various kinds of soup. At one end of the long counter, two women were mixing and making fry bread. As they were dipped out of the oil, they were stacked in a large basket to drain and remain until the meal was ready.

Venison was roasted for several hours, making it tender and succulent, and then sliced and arranged into two large roaster pans. Family, relatives, and friends donated the venison for the memorial service. George brought some scones Isabel had baked that were filled with wild blueberries. This was not unusual to get donations from several sources, especially when the one who had passed was so well known and loved.

Many people were streaming in from various places, mingling, bringing more trinkets to set in the casket. George noticed another Native American flag was folded and snuggled in one corner of the casket. Some of the visitors wore the homemade ribbon shirts. They were bright-colored with contrasting color ribbons. The women had applied a small flower at the top where the ribbon started on the shirt. The men's were plainer but just as colorful.

Many were in full dress regalia with the eagle feathers. Each individually shared good stories, and many leaned in towards the speaker to get every word that was being said. John shared the story about the man and his daughter who came two days prior and how he was so grateful for his life. He told in detail how the departed saved him from the enemy in the war. Many were so pleased to hear everything in detail they smiled and looked proud. Laughter was shared over the stories, which filled the hearts with memories of the past.

Lightfoot walked up to George. "Hey, let's take a walk. We can talk, and I'll have a puff on my pipe."

"Sure, what's on your mind?"

They walked out back where there was less congestion. Lightfoot lit his pipe and puffed a couple times.

"How did the grave-digging go yesterday?" George asked.

"Three of us went with pickaxes and shovels. It took quite a long time to get it done. That ground was frozen solid for over a foot. Good thing it's gravel and sand up there on the hill." Lightfoot pointed with his pipe as he talked.

"So that part is completed and ready?" George asked.

"Yes, and we took Chief with us. He had a certain way he wanted his son to lay."

"I understand. He's taking this really well."

"He had the omen when the white owl came for three days. He said he was ready for something since the first sighting. He prepared his heart from that moment."

George nodded his head. "I have learned from him and have a lot of respect for him."

"George, I'm wondering how you are holding up with this being your friend as well as the tension of not knowing who did this to him."

"I'm doing the best I can. Once today has passed, I will delve into the search for his killer more extensively until I find who it was. Lightfoot, did you notice the guy in there, the one with the greasy hair?"

"Never seen him before today. Why?"

"I haven't either, so what's he doing here? I wonder if he had anything to do with the robbery and murder," George said.

"I figure it has to be someone who overheard about the money or someone curious to the facts surrounding the funeral."

"He could have cleaned up a little. He sticks out like a sore thumb."

"You can never tell about people. The one who did this may not stick out like a sore thumb." Lightfoot knocked the hot coals out of his pipe and said, "Guess we'd better get back in. The priest will arrive soon."

"Priest? I wondered who Chief and Rowena would get for the service."

"Yes, you know, the little church just east of Hessel. This is where the priest comes from. He usually is the one who does this for the tribe."

"I wondered if you would help carry the casket. We, the elders, wish to have you do this."

George choked on an immediate lump in his throat. He swallowed and said, "I would be honored to be a pallbearer with you." He held back tears.

George's parents were walking in the front door as he and Lightfoot entered from the back. George said, "Excuse me, Lightfoot. It's my family."

George quickly regrouped and added a smile, hiding his real feelings. He hugged his mom and shook his dad's hand and then hugged his brother. "I'm glad you're here. Where's that pineapple upside-down cake you made yesterday, Mom?"

"Who told you? I know, it's out in the car. Will you go get it, George?"

"Hey, maybe my brother should. There's an unmarried beauty working in the kitchen today."

"Hush, this is no place to joke about a thing like that," his mother said.

"Okay, he can help me," George said.

Fred raised his eyebrows and followed his brother. "What's her name, George?"

"Penny."

"Okay, here goes. I hope she is more than a good cook if you recommend her."

Reaching the kitchen, George called, "Hey, Penny, I have a cake for you to cut."

"Thank you, *migwetch*." Penny smiled and reached for the cake.

"Penny, I would like you to meet my brother, Fred."

She smiled, holding the cake, and curtsied slightly and then turned away.

"That's it? Now I know her name and have met her…"

"You're on your own." George laughed. The ache in his heart had slightly faded.

The priest had arrived. He was dressed in his black gown with a white collar. His hat was black felt and slightly brimmed. He wore a large gold chain cross that hung and rested on his belly. He held a white leather Bible with gold edging the pages and gold-embossed letters saying, "Holy Bible" on the front. Knowing almost everyone except the visitors from Arizona and Canada, he nodded acknowledgment to them and came to sit near Chief and Rowena.

"Whenever you're ready, I will start the service," he said to Chief.

"There are so many here, yet it has passed the scheduled time. It is best we do start," Chief said.

The crowd became silent when the priest stood up. Many were standing and quickly found a seat. The chairs had been rearranged for all to sit together. George noticed Pierre Bouchard sitting in the back. Jeffery Beacom was there too. Bonnie Dickinson, the bartender, sat with him. Peabody and Tilde sat alone on one side. George sat with his family. Maria had joined them along with Lightfoot. Maria held her camera where she could get a shot of the priest and the casket. George noticed the greasy-haired man sitting near Bouchard.

The priest stood, looked solemnly at the group, cleared his throat, and began. He began by signing the cross and saying, "In the name of the Father, of the Son, and of the Holy Ghost." He looked around and said, "We are gathered today in the presence of our Lord and Savior, Jesus Christ, to pay our last respects to a man who has gone all too soon to be with the Great Spirit, *Gitchi Manitoo*. His departed spirit will not be forgotten for a very long time. His kindness to all who knew him is spread throughout the counties in this area. If anyone ever needed a favor, he was always there helping. He always had a smile on his face, willingly seeing goodness in all mankind. He spent two years in the war, returning highly decorated with war medals. He returned quietly to his home and country and picked up from where he left things as they were before. He was a very humble person, who kept to himself until you spoke to him. No one has a bad word to say against this man. He went from us not by his doing but by the hand of someone else. May God forgive the wrongdoers. We may never know who this person is or persons are, but we must pray for those who were responsible for taking the life of our dear departed and not have harsh feelings towards whoever it was.

"We must keep in mind this service is a celebration of a new journey for his departed soul. We must love and remember him as we have in the past. We must remember the wonderful stories that have been shared here in the past four days. Our life must go on with these memories, knowing he is going on his final journey. Now, please join me in saying the Lord's Prayer together."

"Our Father, who art in heaven, hallowed be thy name, thy kingdom come, thy will be done on earth as it is in heaven. Give us this day our daily bread and forgive us our debts as we forgive our debtors. And lead us not into temptation but deliver us from evil." The priest stopped, but many continued.

"For thine is the kingdom and the power and the glory forever. Amen"

John, the oldest and wisest elder, stood and signaled to Lightfoot and George and to his younger brother, Ken, to come. The room remained silent. The priest stood near and waited, while the elder placed sweet grass *wiingush,* sage *musjodewsk,* tobacco *sema,* and cedar *giizhik* in the casket. He explained, "The four herbs are medicine, *medigan,* indigenous of this area. They represent the four directions, east, west, south, and north." He nodded at John, who closed the casket and nailed it shut. The four lifted the casket and followed the priest to the door where his car was waiting and warmed up. The casket was slid onto the bed of George's truck. Lightfoot rode with George, and John and Ken rode in John's truck; family followed first, and then others followed on down until all who planned to attend the graveside service. Mourners were doubled up in their cars, so there was room enough at the cemetery.

The procession would go north to Dixie Highway past the Runway Bar west to the Italian cemetery. When they passed the little grocery store, George noticed it was closed and a wreath hung on the door. A few yards farther, a wreath also hung on Hanson Garage. They both attended the funeral with their wives and remained at the community hall.

As the procession arrived at the grave site, the priest stood with the mourners to one side. The pipe carrier smoked his pipe. Everyone would use the community pipe. They passed it around and was offered to all except those women who were in the moon cycle. The smoke went to the Great Spirit, *Gitchi Manitoo,* cleansing the way for the great journey.

Respectfully, they would not utter his name for a while so as not to interrupt his journey.

The casket was lowered. Many walked past and said good-bye, *bamapii,* before they returned to the hall for the great feast.

George waited for all who passed the grave. His heart was heavy. This was the final good-bye, *bamapii,* for George and his friend. His shoulders shook; all that he had held in for the past two weeks released from his body. Still, he remained quiet, holding back the loud cry that erupted in his throat. He replaced his hat on his head and turned away from the best friend he ever had. George promised quietly he would get the one who was responsible for taking his best friends' life.

——————

The hall was rearranged with tables and chairs lined up for the families and friends to eat. The crowd had dwindled after the service at the hall. Many went home after the priest left; however, there were approximately one hundred people that stayed for the celebration later.

A place setting was saved between Chief and Rowena, as was and an empty chair for their departed son. The pipe carrier returned thanks for the meal, and one table at a time filed up to the buffet to fill their plates.

The buffet table had two huge electric roasters at the end full of venison; there were buffalo meatballs, potatoes, wild rice, squash, corn soup, corn bread and fry bread, pickled eggs, and too many desserts to choose from.

Isabel walked in with her friends, Veronica and Veronica's husband, Keith, who both worked with her at the school.

They met George halfway across the room. "What a pleasant surprise. Come join us at the table where I am sitting. I'll arrange three more chairs. In fact, join the line at the buffet table while I get your chairs."

Isabel had changed clothes and came with her friends who had changed at George's home before coming. He was proud to see Isabel in her church dress.

Lightfoot leaned over and said in a low voice, "I know Veronica and her husband, Keith. They are distant relatives."

"Isabel works with them. Isabel and Veronica are close," George said. "They gave her a ride out here after work."

Returning with their plates full, George showed them the three chairs and helped Isabel seat herself. They began eating and talking amongst themselves.

"How did the funeral go, George?" asked Isabel.

"It was a good day," George answered. "Isabel, will you stay with me until I can leave tonight?"

"I'd rather not because I will be working here tomorrow cleaning things up, and I'm really tired after the long day at work."

"Are your friends driving you home?"

"Of course, they always give me a ride when I need it. Really, George, they are very good friends."

"I see. That's good. I will try to get home as soon as possible."

"We'll be leaving as soon as we finish eating. I thought it would be good to make a showing, at least."

"Yes, you're right to do this. Don't forget to speak to my folks and Chief and Rowena before you leave."

"I will. I'll see you when you arrive home." She pecked is cheek with a kiss.

George was slightly miffed. It would have been better if she had not come as late as it was. He noticed a strange look on his mother's face as she looked in Isabel's direction, but who could tell what she was thinking?

Isabel went over to speak to Mr. and Mrs. Kaughman and Fred. They shook hands. Then she went over to Chief and Rowena and, in a low voice, spoke to them. They smiled in response. Isabel and her friends left shortly after.

"Son, this was a very good ceremony. The food was excellent, but now we must leave to do the chores," George's father said.

George shook his hand and hugged his mother and brother.

Fredrick went to Penny's side and shook her hand. "It was nice to meet you. Maybe we will see each other in different circumstances and have a nice talk."

Penny smiled and agreed. "Yes, it was and yes. Bye." Fred looked back as he left and almost stumbled over a chair.

"I'll be leaving as soon as I have the tables folded and chairs stacked. I sure am glad you came today. I love you. See you soon," George said to his parents.

"Thank you for coming and for the delicious cake too," Lightfoot said to George's family. "I'll stay and help George with the stacking of the tables and chairs."

"How kind of you," Mrs. Kaughman said. "You have been a great help for George, and we appreciate what you have done."

Soon everyone had left except for the ladies in the kitchen, George and Lightfoot.

Marie left when Isabel came in. She had work to do at the press office—photos to develop, a story to write, and a breath of fresh air.

CHAPTER TWENTY

It Was a Good Day

As George left the hall, he heard one old man reminiscing with another while they walked home. One was hard of hearing and partially blind at the age of ninety-seven. They walked slowly and recalled the events of the day. Their conversation through the woods echoed back to George.

The younger of the two talked loudly so the elder could hear him because he missed out on much of the conversation. "It was a good day. To the people from the area, he was a war hero. This alone was enough to bring many to show their last respects. Many came to view him. They sat around and exchanged stories, things they had done together. Some were funny, while other stories were serious. All were good to repeat. Prior to today, the final day, many wild blueberry scones were baked and stored for use as needed. Wild rice was being prepared for the last meal, and soon the ladies were ready for the eating. From the kitchen, they could hear the singing of long and beautiful songs. I heard another story told about him by his uncle from Canada. The sharing began at ten in the morning. The fire keeper kept the fire going throughout the entire mourning period in honor of the final ceremony. As the visitors passed to view his casket, it was not surprising to see an eagle feather placed in the casket, guaranteeing a safe journey. Some would give a gift back to him. His war medals were placed along with the tribal flag. Then everyone was in the wigwam, including the ladies who were cooking. The pipe carrier was chosen because he is wise, a leader, one who keeps a straight and narrow path and carries out many obligations, and honorable. He stepped out in the door, *ishkwaandem* is what he is called."

"Ya, I know," said the elder.

"Almost everyone had gathered once more in the wigwam. Some had stayed there throughout the day. Some were in the hall. All were silent. The pipe carrier, the ceremonial person, lit the pipe and let the smoke rise to the Great Spirit, *Gitchi Manitoo*, guiding his spirit home. Nothing but silence ensued for a long peaceful time." They had stopped to rest and talk about this day. "It was a good day," they said again. Then they continued walking. Later Lightfoot and George were walking behind the Great Hall and up from the wigwam. The sun felt good in the late afternoon.

Lightfoot looked down over the cliff to the cedar swamp that was fifty feet below and said, "Funny, I thought I could see him go down the trail to check his traps."

George answered, "Could have, it was a beautiful memorial service. I heard them say it. They are two great men."

"I agree with you, my friend."

George heard the voices of the two men until they faded out of hearing range. He smiled. He knew this was how the story would begin and would go on from these few words to a great good day for a funeral.

CHAPTER TWENTY-ONE

A Flat Tire

It was dark by the time George left for home. He had driven about a mile when the truck began to wobble. He realized he had a flat tire. Pulling over to the side, he reached in back of the seat for the tire iron. It wasn't there. He took his flashlight and looked under the seats to no avail. He hiked about a mile to the nearest home and asked for assistance. The man knew him and helped George put on the spare.

"Thanks for your help, Dave. I owe you one."

"No, that was my pleasure. You don't owe me anything."

George decided to get the tire fixed the next day. It was late and time to relax before turning in for the night.

The house appeared to be dark when George pulled into the yard. *Isabel must have gone to bed*, George thought.

He entered to find the lights out and an empty bed.

CHAPTER TWENTY-TWO

A Talk with Wendell Peabody

The sound of a horn woke George from a very sound sleep. After the long eventful ceremony and burial of Two Shoes the day before, George was physically and emotionally drained. He slept so sound he didn't hear Isabel come in and wasn't sure what hour it was. It took a while for him to fall asleep, but the last thing he remembered was that it was two in the afternoon.

The sun shined through the eastern bedroom window. George jumped to his feet to see who was honking outside. From the front room window, he saw Victoria sitting in her automobile, an old 35 Ford, waiting expectantly for Isabel. Isabel also roused from a deep sleep at the sound of the horn honking. "It's Victoria, she is taking me to the hall to clean up after the funeral. Last evening, she asked to be included on the crew for the job." Isabel called to George. She remained in bed while he went to build the fire.

George thought he remembered Isabel asking to remind Sally she and Victoria would come to clean up the day after the funeral.

"I'll wave to her to let her know you heard the horn beeping," George called over his shoulder after he had pulled his pants on and went to the window to wave her in. He quickly added wood to the stove and then went to the bedroom to pull on a shirt and a pair of socks.

He heard the coffeepot bang on the burner of the range as Isabel scooped coffee into it.

Victoria walked in and said, "Forgot what time you wanted to go, so I came the same time we start at school each morning."

"Make yourself at home, Victoria," George said. "Coffee will be ready in a flash."

Victoria looked at George and took off her coat but left her boots on.

"We can have coffee first. Sit down, Victoria. There is ample time before we have to leave," Isabel said as she began cooking eggs and pancakes. George got the maple syrup out and checked the woodstove to see if it was burning okay. He poked a couple sticks of kindling in to help it burn more quickly.

"George, all this smoke! Open the damper." Isabel scolded.

"Uh-oh, say can you see…" George sang, "by the dawns early…"

"Okay, okay, we'll be out of here soon." Isabel interrupted, grinning.

"Make some pancakes for me too," George said.

"I am. Just help by setting the table, please. It'll be ready in a jiffy."

George noticed she had quickly piled pancakes on a platter and that the eggs were ready too. He grabbed the butter and syrup, placed them on the table, and they all sat down to eat. George returned thanks while all heads were bowed.

"You know, spring is only fifty days away. Soon we can take liberty to watch for green grass," Victoria said.

"I saw a pair of hawks eating on a skunk the other day. That's a sign of spring too."

"George, not at the breakfast table!"

George laughed, and Victoria joined in.

"Green grass, what is it? It's been so long I forgot," Isabel remarked.

"Each spring for ten years, you have said the same thing," George said.

"Yes, and for ten years, I have wondered if I would ever get away from this terrible snow-covered region," Isabel said with a scowl.

"And each spring when the wind comes from the south bringing snow melting and the fresh smell of earth, you wrinkle up your face and say, 'I have spring fever.'" He took a quick breath and added, "Perhaps we can do something soon if you can take time away for a week or so." George consoled her.

"I'll cover for you, Isabel, when you go. I'm sure Peabody will be willing. He knows what a hard worker you are."

"We'll see how things go. Thanks, Victoria."

With the last swallow of coffee down, Victoria pushed back her chair, checked the clock, and said, "We need to leave."

"You're right. George, would you clean up?" Isabel asked.

"Sure, honey, my schedule is slow and relaxing today."

George heard Victoria's car start, the muffler roaring until it was out of sight. He checked the woodstove once again before he began cleaning the breakfast table and washing the dishes. He stood at the kitchen sink, thinking what his plans actually were for the day. He would have to have the tire repaired. He wanted to look for the tire iron, which he thought he must have misplaced in the garage. He forgot to ask Isabel if she had seen it. Then, after the tire was fixed, he would go down to the office for a short while.

With his shirtsleeves rolled up and hands in suds, he washed the dishes, rinsed, and piled them on the sink to drain. He wiped down the table and chair seats, drained the water, and hung the dishcloth to dry. He swept the floor and put the broom and dustpan back on the porch next to the cooler.

Another thaw promised as George checked the thermometer with the mercury rising to thirty-four degrees. He rolled his sleeves down, buttoned the cuffs, and pulled on his heavy coat. He grabbed his hat and gloves as he went out the front door.

Instead of going to the garage to fix the tire, George decided to walk up his street and turned left at the corner to Peabody's home. Peabody would be home at this hour, and George was determined to ask him about being with Alice last fall. He walked east up the street and left a short way and then right to Peabody's home on the hill across from the school. Although it was close, the pines, cedars, cabins, and a couple homes obstructed the view from his place. When he turned the corner, George saw Peabody was home. He stomped his feet to remove the snow and announced his arrival at the same time. Peabody answered the door with a surprised look on his face.

"Hello, Wendell, I have been talking to witnesses, and a question has come up about something that was seen last fall, something that includes you."

Peabody's face turned bright red. "What might that be about?"

"I believe you know, but I'll come right out with it. Wendell…"

"Here, George, come into my office," Wendell interrupted.

He opened the door and ushered George in. "Take a seat." Wendell Peabody seated himself behind his desk where he sat on the edge of his seat.

"See here, Wendell, the story you told me earlier and what I have heard recently simply conflict."

Wendell sat mute and waited for George to continue.

"You told a very sad story about your true love that made me almost feel sorry for you. Now I've been told you saw her as recent as this past fall. Only two and a half months ago. I have a sworn statement from your witness to that effect. What do you have to say about this?"

Wendell hesitated for a moment. "It's true, George, but I didn't think you would need to know this fact."

"I wouldn't need to know? How can a man solve a crime if no one is willing to tell the whole facts? You tell me, and I'll decide if the truth is necessary." George was disgusted.

"Okay, Alice did come to see me last fall. She had just returned from spending a lengthy stay in Oregon, where she visited the hot springs. The spa there healed her after a period of time. She underwent therapy and rehabilitation. After several months, she realized she was well enough to return home. That was when she came to visit me.

We went to a secluded spot where we could talk. I was so excited and nervous at the same time. She pledged her love to me again, and we promised each other we would be together by the end of school year. When she left, I wasn't sure how I would tell Tilde, but I figured I'd think of something by May. Now, after the robbery, I couldn't bribe Tilde with some of the money, and I really do need the bonds back. It's all up in the air." Wendell Peabody was pulling on his thinning hair, and then he began to pace the floor.

"That's it? Did it occur to you Alice could have gotten cold feet and hired someone or robbed you herself?"

"Never! Our feelings for each other is a once-in-a-lifetime bond. Nothing could sever that feeling."

"Wendell, I hope you do work your situation out and that everyone involved can be happy."

George stood and continued, "That does clarify your part of this mystery. You have proven to me your love is sound, and I feel badly for Tilde. My best to you and your life. I'll do whatever I can to help get the bonds and money back. I feel so close to how this came about, but there are a couple clues that hasn't been revealed to me yet. I'm going to fix my flat first today, and then I'll begin working on the remaining clues."

A look of relief spread across Peabody's face. He stood and shook George's hand. "Let me walk with you for a short distance. I'm going over to the school for a while."

"To call Alice."

"Yes."

CHAPTER TWENTY-THREE

Alarming Discovery

At first, George had planned to get the tire fixed at Hanson's garage, and then he decided to find his tire iron and try to fix it himself. After all the experience he had on the farm, this was an easy chore.

Normally, Isabel or he would enter through the side door of the garage, unless it was necessary to open the wide doors to park the truck. He turned the latch on the two garage doors that folded and latched at the center when he closed it. He forcibly pulled on them against the snow that accumulated in front of the doors. While pushing the snow away, his eyes fell on a track in the snow that was crow-shaped. George frowned. *Strange*, he thought. Brown lines through the crow-foot-shaped track settled in the V-shaped groove. It was very similar to the one at Peabody's backyard and also at the murder scene. Was this a joke? Or was it just a coincidence? Finally, the doors were open enough to gain entrance from that vantage point.

It was impossible to see at first until his eyes focused on the dimly lighted garage. A dim light came when the sun shined through the three small dirty windows along the south wall. He began looking for a tire iron or a wrench that would fit the nuts on his tire somewhere on the bench. It was heavily covered with dust and cobwebs. On top were a few nails, a wire brush, and a pair of pliers. Looking up along the wall where he hung the pliers and wire brush, he checked the various types of hammers, screwdrivers, wrenches, saws, paintbrushes, and other tools. The tire iron wasn't there either.

He hung the plyers on the space chosen for it, reached for the wire brush, and also hung it up.

Under the bench were cardboard boxes of old rags, buckets of nails, and screws. Small wooden boxes of nuts and bolts in assorted sizes sat on a two-by-ten board. His coal bucket sat at the end where he kept it to empty the ashes from the woodstove in the cabin. His eyes looked back along the entire wall, bench, and under when his eye rested on a box of rags. He pawed his way through the rags. Suddenly, his hand hit against something solid—a soiled tire iron sticking to a rag with brown stains. *Oh, for Lord's sake*, he thought, *it can't be*. He dizzily caught himself as he momentarily swooned. There was no doubt that the stains were blood. If George was wrong, he would be happier than not. *Was this his tire iron? Was it planted in his garage? Who used it? Not Isabel, not me. Was Jeffery trying to mislead me?*

There was little doubt this wasn't the murder weapon. Brown stains in the snow. Wiping it off the tire iron could make a crow-shaped print. Whoever did use the tire iron also used it or something similar to it behind Peabody's house as well as on the ice at the murder scene. George made his way to the cabin, went in, and sat in his chair concentrating for a while. His head whirled while his thoughts shot in several directions. He reflected the many moves he made in the last few days before the murder, and even before then. Who in the community would be so hateful that they would kill his very best friend and plant the murder weapon in his garage? The convicting evidence was here right before his eyes, and he had to think straight about how it got there and why. If it was Isabel, why would she? It couldn't be.

He thought longer. He thought about the past ten years, how the marriage with Isabel was good at first, but now, she was distant more and more. She spent a lot of time with Virginia and working overtime. Or was she working overtime? He realized he had worked long hours and often went to the Cedarville Bar after hours. He had never asked about her paycheck or how much she earned. He tried to be home near to or as soon as she came home or, at least, return before supper was ready. He placed his hand on his forehead and pressed it as though the thoughts could become gone, that they would just disappear. When he opened his eyes, he was looking at the shelf where Isabel lined up her precious collection. Her only joy was to collect something new every time she saw something different. He looked at her collection as though he were seeing it for the first time. Birds, bears, cats, dogs, a moose, horse, and even a model Ford Model T automobile; each one was unique in some way and usually was made of various materials, some of hand-carved wood, some were porcelain pottery, and some were...*onyx*!

CHAPTER TWENTY-FOUR

One Step Closer

"Sheeaat! Good Grief. It can't be." George planted both feet on the floor and stood erect with both eyes looking straight at the shelf full of Isabel's collection of figurines. A close scrutiny revealed each and every figurine was coated with dust, grease film from cooking, stains of cigarette, and wood smoke except one. This one was nearly without dirt, the onyx bear.

He sat down in shock and thought soundly. It did resemble the description Peabody gave of the onyx bear that was in the safe. It was the statue his sweetheart gave him. The sweetheart that intended to run away with Peabody. The sweetheart that was injured in an accident and couldn't walk, so she broke up with Peabody. Yet she was seen again after that and was walking very well last fall just before the first snowfall. "All along, I've barked up the wrong tree. The bait was here all along," George said out loud.

For two weeks, George could have seen it. It sat there right before his eyes, but he never looked at anything Isabel liked. He overlooked what he was searching for while beating at his brain, wondering who did it, always thinking about who may have taken it to sell for more money. He had wondered who heard about the money and robbed the safe of everything, including the bonds and onyx figurine of a tiny bear.

All the while, it stood in his home. All the while, his wife...*Did I talk in my sleep? I can't believe it is her. God, help me. Please don't let it be her.* George thought while he held his head with both hands. *How could I have been so blind?*

Then it dawned on him, Isabel was at the reservation, at the hall. She planned to clean up the hall after the funeral ceremony from the day before. "I must go get her. I must confront her with what I found."

George gathered his keys, coat, hat, and gloves again and drove nearly blind with emotion towards the reservation. His heart was bursting from within. He swerved away from an oncoming truck while driving in blind fury. He almost hit a mailbox and straightened the truck while he tried to shake off this blind rage. "My wife, I can't believe it was her."

He reached the hall, parked his pickup, and rushed into the great room. He slammed the door loudly against the wall.

"Victoria, where is Isabel?" he shouted loudly so everyone could hear him.

"She's out back having a smoke," Victoria answered with a surprised look on her face.

George walked quickly out the back door to see Isabel backing away from Robert Lightfoot and Chief, Two Shoes' father. Her mouth was open in horror. Her long curly dark hair flew in disarray. Her eyes were on Lightfoot and Chief as she backed within inches of the cliff, which dropped fifty feet down into the swamp. George could tell by what he saw that Lightfoot and Chief knew. They had figured out who had killed Two Shoes.

Instead of taking her into custody, they planned an accident, George speculated. An accident that could get revenge for the tribe and save George from extra heartache. With this plan, they hoped he would never know the truth.

George lunged forward and hoped to catch her in time. Just as she took the final step backwards over the cliff, George caught her in his arms. "Isabel!" George shouted as they rolled to safety in the snow.

She looked at him with a dazed expression. "George, I can explain it all."

"And that you will, my dear." George spoke in a cold tone. "You are under arrest for the murder of Two Shoes."

CHAPTER TWENTY-FIVE

An Unexpected Event

George cuffed Isabel and started towards the car.

"Wait," called Lightfoot, striding close behind George.

"What is it, Lightfoot?"

Chief had caught up and stood next to Lightfoot.

Lightfoot looked at John, the elder who was always there and ready to help in any situation. "John, will you take Isabel to the truck while I talk to the sheriff?"

"Sure, I will." He gestured to Isabel to go ahead while he followed

"You remember that fellow you asked about yesterday? The one with greasy hair and a blue-and-white plaid flannel shirt?"

"Yes, I do. Why?"

"When Isabel and her friends entered yesterday during the meal, he looked her way and got up and left. The men including John saw him and followed. He left on an Eliason snowmobile machine."

"I did see that he was gone. So the men followed him? Why?"

"He didn't reveal who he was, but he acted suspicious. I told them to follow him. I'm sorry, George, I should have told you. I should have told you last night, but you needed a good rest."

"What do you mean? What are you getting at, Lightfoot?"

"It's complicated. John and Frank grabbed a couple snow machines and headed after him. He went north. They didn't hear him turn west on Dixie Highway, so they assumed he kept heading north. It took a few minutes before they could see him again. He was at least two miles ahead. You know those Eliason snow machines go like hell, at least sixty miles per hour. He kept heading north and acted like he didn't realize the two were behind him. Suddenly, he headed east, following the Dixie Highway out to the main road north heading towards Pickford or Sault Ste. Marie. When they reached the second turn, he was well ahead of them. They both knew they would have to speed up to catch him. Finally, he turned around and saw them approaching. He gunned his sleigh ahead. He flew through Pickford without slowing down. The space between him and John and Frank began widening. The pursuit seemed to discourage Frank, he slowed down. John wouldn't give up. By now, John was sure you and I had a good reason to suspect the guy."

John had walked up while Lightfoot was talking to George. "That's right, but I would like to tell the remaining part in private, if it's possible," John said, looking over to where Isabel and Chief stood next to George's truck.

Lightfoot said, "I don't think she can hear us talking, but we can go into the hall while you talk to John."

Chief stayed with Isabel in the truck.

George turned to John and said, "Okay, John, tell me what happened next."

"So, as Lightfoot was saying, things seemed almost impossible for us to catch up to this guy. The Great Spirit intervened, and I give him praise. All of a sudden, the sleigh ahead of me began to slow down. The creep tried to turn into an open field. Even though the Eliason machines are fast, they can't turn worth a hoot. Suddenly, it slowed down and stopped. I caught up to him as he lit out across the field on foot, fighting the deep snow. I headed my machine right after him. When I was alongside him, I jumped from my machine and bulldozed him. All I had was a rope in the toolbox to tie him up, so that's what I used. Then I tied him to his sleigh and towed him back to Pickford. I stopped at Slater's gas station and called the hall where Lightfoot waited. I saw Frank waited for me at the station also. I was relieved to know he would help me keep him under control. He whined about how he didn't understand why we came after him. Then I told him to be quiet."

154

"What happened next?"

"Well, Lightfoot arrived and put him in the backseat and took him to the hall. We followed and arrived back a few minutes later. Then Lightfoot asked him what he was doing at the funeral dinner. He said he wanted a free meal. Lightfoot called him a liar and began to get rough with him. Lightfoot asked what his name was and where he came from. He finally said he was from Newberry but that his sister lived east of Cedarville. He also added that he and his sister were *anishnaabe* and that they shouldn't be treated this way. He said they were brothers by blood. This made Lightfoot angrier. He searched his pockets and found his name with his driver's license. When he searched his snow machine he found a bag of money. It appeared to be a very large amount, but we didn't count it. Lightfoot has it, he plans to give it to you."

"Thank you, John, I'll take Isabel home and turn her in in the morning."

George reached the truck where Chief and Isabel sat with the engine running to keep them warm. Lightfoot followed George to his truck with the money sack in his hand.

"Thanks, Chief. I'll take her home and head over in the morning to the county jail."

"Excuse me, George, this is one time I am going to interfere. I believe I should go with you since she is your wife. I also believe we should go directly to the jail right now."

George thought for a brief second, half-smiled, and said, "You're right, Lightfoot. If you drive, I will have a chance to talk to Isabel and get some answers from her."

CHAPTER TWENTY-SIX

A Revelation

Lightfoot slid behind the wheel of the Ford pickup. Isabel was in the middle and George on the window. They rode silently away from the hall.

Isabel suddenly broke the silence. "So you're taking me to jail."

"Yes, you have broken the laws of this world as well as God's law. We need to talk. I need to get an explanation from you, something we can document as a confession when we get to the county sheriff's office."

Isabel remained silent. George looked sideways at her, waiting. They continued west. The only sound was the snow hitting under the truck. George knew he always kept blank report forms behind the seat in a briefcase in case of an emergency. He reached back and grabbed his briefcase. He needed to hear the reason why it was necessary for Isabel to kill his friend.

"Look at me, Isabel. I need to look straight into your eyes while you answer my questions. If you wish to explain your side of this sordid affair, I will listen. I will not interrupt you until you have finished, but I do have questions to ask, and I intend to get the answers."

"George, it starts way back, ten years ago, when you found me in Lansing that night. I had been supporting myself by prostituting ever since I ran away from home at the age of sixteen."

Lightfoot cleared his throat, letting George know he was regret-fully witnessing everything she said, and decidedly would not show surprise at her words.

"I wanted a better life. It even goes farther back to the fact when my dad was a maintenance man at AC Spark Plug factory in Flint and the family of seven was more than my father could provide for. We never had anything. I wore old hand-me-downs and secondhand shoes. In spite of my secondhand attire, I was attractive and clean. At the age of thirteen, I sold my body for twenty dollars more than once. The word spread fast, and I was the object of gossip. That's when I ran away with money I stole from my mother's purse. I caught a ride on Highway M-21, and when I finally reached Lansing, I had exactly twenty dollars. That's when I started being selective. Before long, I had senators and other wealthy clients. By the time I was twenty years old, I discovered this was not the answer. I yearned for a good life with the right man. I read in the state journal about the upcom-ing conventions and began hanging at the convention hall. I dressed in the best of clothing, which enabled me to mix in that type of crowd and be accepted. Repeatedly, I would look for 'Mister Right.' Then you came along and swept me off my feet. I was in love for the very first time in my life."

"Spare me the sweet talk, please," George said. His heart had hardened since he was sure without a doubt she was the culprit.

Isabel continued, "All the excitement of moving to the Upper Peninsula, being the wife of the local sheriff, prestige all changed. The excitement for me from the wedding, along with a long automo-bile trip to Mackinaw City and the scary ferry ride across the straits, and then all the dusty gravel roads to Cedarville to the tiny cabin you lived in broke my bubble. My dream of a fancy sheriff's mansion was crushed. Not to mention you were just a deputy sheriff overseeing this rural area. My disappointment was so great that I knew I had to get a job, save up, and soon get away from this god-forsaken place. The ice-cold floors in the winter, never going anywhere, and nothing to do besides work, cook, clean house, and be the good wife, they became old very soon. Yet I stayed, hoping I would have a child or something to fill the void in my life."

George cleared his throat and interrupted, "Don't you think I wanted a child too? Let's get to the facts. All these things are just an excuse for the crime you committed."

"Don't get in a hurry, George. It's my time to tell it the way it was. The honeymoon was over, and I was looking for comfort. Two Shoes would stop in to see me from time to time. You were always gone."

"That's a lie. I don't believe you." Now George knew what Jeffery Beacom held back, the other affair that was going on. It made him sick.

Isabel continued, "He knew when you were gone, and he knew when you would return, so don't question it. I liked the attention he gave me. He wasn't handsome, was of short build, but he had a smile that never faded. He even carved a wooden trinket and gave it to me. I kept it on my shelf. You never noticed. I was infatuated with the idea that he cared for me. It wasn't love, but I looked forward to the times he stopped in. Then he went to war, and you still kept away all those long hours."

"Victoria has a brother. He came over from time to time from Newberry and stayed for a couple days. Victor is Victoria's twin brother. He was my new friend, someone to listen to my problems."

"Two Shoes told me about the money. He was headed to the bar but stopped in here first. He couldn't wait to tell someone, and because he always stopped if you weren't home, he spilled his guts and told everything he saw. A lightbulb went on in my head. Peabody's money was precisely what I needed to get away. I barely realized Two Shoes had left, yet I faintly remember he gave me a squeeze as he went out the door.

"I planned all night and got very little sleep. I planned to go to Peabody's home the next night while he was at the school board meeting. Tilde always went to her card game with her lady friends, so it would be the best time to do it. Two Shoes stopped in right after I returned home from my job at the school. He said you were joining him at Cedarville Bar. I hugged him and said to have a good time at the bar. Darkness came just a half hour later. I quickly dressed in a pair of black slacks, a sweatshirt, and a black hooded jacket. Leaving the house through the back door, I cautiously sought my way over and across the road to Peabody's house. Keeping to the trees and shrubbery, I kept my back to the wall around the house up the three steps to the back door. I took the tire iron with me to pry the door open. It didn't take much, the old wood was rotten, and it gave way to my third try. Once in the house, I found my way to the bedroom. The safe was just as Two Shoes described it, at the foot of the bed under the table cover that shielded it from view. It took longer to pry the safe open, but finally it sprung open."

"The safe was full with money, just as Two Shoes said. I shoved it into my canvas schoolbag. Underneath, I discovered the onyx figurine of a bear. I had to have it. I took it and wrapped it with some papers that lay at the bottom of the safe. I stuffed the figurine in my pouch in front of my sweatshirt, and I hid the bag of money inside my shirt next to my skin. The flashlight and tire iron were easily pocketed in my baggy pants after I rubbed the wood splinters that stuck to the iron."

"I pulled my hood back over my head and shadowed my face in case I met anyone on my way back to the cabin. I took the main street and then cut across and over to the cabin. The wind blew so hard I had to keep my head down to protect my face. Blowing from the east, I believed I could hear music, but it was just my nerves. It dawned on me that the papers in the safe could lead to my destruction and ruin my plans, so I unwrapped the figurine and put it back in my pouch. The wind caught the papers and blew them every which way. I just let them go and hustled towards the cabin. I arrived home before you and hid the tire iron in the garage. I didn't want to hide the onyx bear, so I put it among my collection on the shelf."

"That was your first mistake, Isabel. Strange too because I didn't plan to meet Two Shoes that night. I had gone out to the farm to get fresh milk," George said. "Where did you hide the money?"

"No interruptions, remember?"

"No, I need to know what you did with that money." George pressed her for an answer.

"I hid it in a safe place. I knew if you found it, it was crackers for me. Later I gave it to Victor. He was planning to run away with me when the time was right."

"You are fickle. What was he going to do to help you get away? Where is the money right now?"

"I don't know for sure. I'll have to talk to Victor. But now you are taking me to the county sheriff's office, so you will have the job of finding where the money is."

"Tell me why you felt you needed to murder Two Shoes."

"I took the money, and momentarily I felt free. Free to leave this hellhole of a place, to make a new life, and to have the things I longed for. But then I began to love the little onyx bear figure more than the freedom the money could bring me. I took it down each day and held it.

"My freedom was again robbed from me because Two Shoes stopped over to check on me, and I held my breath, fearing he would look up and see my new trinket. If he saw it, he would know where I got it and know I was the one who robbed Peabody."

"After thinking how I could avoid this encounter, I began making plans to murder him. I had to kill him. Don't you see? He would make me give everything back, and I wouldn't be able to get away. I thought, how could I do this? Where and when should I choose to end his life? He must go not only because of my needing freedom but also because he robbed me of your time to the point that I sought a new companion in Victor. Then I worked out a new plan. My plan was to kill Two Shoes and leave with Victor."

Isabel sat between Lightfoot and George with her arms crossed against her chest. George merely looked at her in horror. "Who are you? I don't even know you."

Isabel looked away and continued, "That Friday, I saw Two Shoes walk past the cabin and head in the direction of the channel. In spite of the cold, the sun was shining. I knew I would have to take caution and not let Smith see me, so I waited until near dusk. I wore my black hooded jacket and took the back trail along the edge of the swamp behind Bay Drive weaving between the dead cattails. It wasn't long before I crept across the road onto the ice where Two Shoes stood fishing. He looked up and said, 'What are you doing here?' I told him that I came to make him promise not to tell about anything he saw. He looked surprised and said, 'What are you talking about?' Then I lunged for Two Shoes. When he took a step backwards, he stumbled, slipped, and fell. I pulled the tire iron out of the pouch on my hooded jacket and slammed it hard on his head. His eyes rolled, and he looked at me with a dazed glassy incomprehensive look. I hit him again and again until I knew he was unconscious or dead. I slipped him into his fishing trench in the ice feetfirst. The deed was done. I wiped most of the blood off the tire iron in the snow and scurried back on the trail home. No one saw me, I was free."

George looked straight into her face and slowly spoke. "Isabel, Jesus said in John chapter eight, verse twenty-two, 'You shall know the truth, and the truth shall set you free.' That was for the believers." *She doesn't understand, yet she appears to show some remorse. Jeffery tried to tell me she was seeing someone else. Did he know about both Two Shoes and Victor as well?*

George continued, "I found your hooded jacket and the tire iron yesterday in the box of rags under the work bench in the garage." He paused for a moment and then continued, "We have caught Victor and have retrieved the money or part of it. It will be returned to Mr. Peabody. Victor was escaping north yesterday. I believe he planned to head to Newberry. Did you know anything about this?"

"I don't believe you. He wouldn't do that to me. He promised we could leave for Lower Michigan and a new life." Isabel continued, "Being down below, life is more exciting. We could have had gone anywhere without traveling very far to get there. We could do every-thing. You said he was headed to Newberry?"

"Life down below certainly will be more than exciting in an everlasting fire," George retorted.

"Lightfoot, can I talk to Victor when we get to the jail?" Isabel asked.

"Isabel, what are you thinking? Don't you know? He left with the snow sled yesterday. Without you. I don't think he wants to talk to you."

CHAPTER TWENTY-SEVEN

A Dreaded Journey

Lightfoot pulled the truck up to the county jail located in the basement of the courthouse. The three-foot rock and cement walls could not be penetrated. In the history of this jail, no one had ever escaped.

George helped Isabel out of the passenger's side. Lightfoot followed the two as they walked into the courthouse and down the steps.

"What do we have here?" the young deputy asked.

"This is Isabel Kaughman. She is under arrest for murder."

"Who did she murder?" the deputy asked.

"Byron 'Two Shoes' Running Bear."

"That rings a bell. I do remember you called in a murder a few days ago. I'll take her in the holding room while we fill out the papers to document your report."

Deputy Paquin unlocked the double thick steel door and then escorted Isabel into the small room adjacent to the main room. She followed silently with her head down. The room was plain with only a narrow cot, a pillow and blanket, a chair in the corner, and the only light came from the lightbulb hanging with a pull chain. George heard the door slam loudly as Deputy Paquin returned to the two waiting men.

"You're saying the war hero, Two Shoes?"

George answered, "Yes, and my best friend. He never hurt anyone, and he didn't deserve this."

"Okay, start from the moment you first discovered Two Shoes' body up to the point where you believe she is the one that murdered him."

George told the deputy all he could remember, who he had suspected, the questions and answers that were supplied from each suspect or witness, and how he found clues that led him to the discovery that Isabel was the murderer. Deputy Paquin had turned on the tape recorder, a detailed report of each step of the investigation, including anything Lightfoot added during the time George found the tire iron, which brought the investigation to a climax.

The deputy looked at Lightfoot and asked, "What, if anything more, can you add to this?"

"First of all, like George has said, I was asked to join in on the investigation. Since Two Shoes is Native American, George believed it would be better for a member of the tribe to become involved as well. Yesterday the elders and I caught a man with a very large amount of money. We arrested him and brought him in last evening."

"Oh yes, so there definitely is a connection between the two?"

"We discovered he has been seeing Isabel. They were planning to run away with the money. It appears he decided to leave without her."

"What does this have to do with the murder? Was he involved?"

"He was willing to run away with her, and then it appears he became greedy and wanted all the money."

"Okay, it is beginning to fit together. We can question him again now that we have more information."

George handed the statement Isabel made on the ride over to the deputy. "If you need anything else, you can contact us, and we will be happy to help. I think we have told everything we know, right, Lightfoot?"

"Yup."

"Well, it took long enough to get all the details of this report. It's one o'clock in the morning," the deputy said.

"If you have further questions, call tomorrow." George spoke to the deputy as he and Lightfoot turned to leave.

The two were beginning to ascend the steps when George heard the deputy yell. "What in hell—oh, for Lord's sake…"

It was coming from the holding room. "George, Lightfoot, come back here."

Apparently, when Deputy Paquin went in to move Isabel into a cell where she would stay until her hearing in the courtroom upstairs, he found her.

When George entered the room, he looked up at the steam pipe from the furnace. His eyes followed the knotted sheet down to Isabel's neck where her head and body hung limply. One agonized word bellowed out of George, "Noooooooo!"

His anguished cry echoed throughout the area.

He rushed to Isabel, wrapped his arms around the lower part of her body, and raised her up to release the pressure. Her body was cold and stiff. Her hair had turned snow white. It was fate; it was meant to be. She had given him ten years of companionship, and now it was over.

He got to his feet and steadily backed away.

CHAPTER TWENTY-EIGHT

The Real Culprit

The men left the building with heavy hearts, especially George who finally realized he could be a poor judge of character. He beat himself up inwardly but not for long; reason told him differently. She had her place in life, which was far from what anyone could possibly fathom. In spite of being a hard worker, good cook, and appearing to be a good wife, there was a dark side of her that was finally revealed.

Deputy Paquin reached out to George and shook his hand. "I'm really sorry you had to see this, but I felt it better now than later."

Lightfoot stood without motion or speech. George returned the handshake, turned on his heel, and headed up the stairs, bent on leaving. Lightfoot followed.

Deputy Paquin watched the men leave the building and dialed up the county sheriff. "I believe you need to be here, sir. We have a situation."

"What could be so bad you need to call me after one in the morning, Paquin?"

"Deputy Sheriff George Kaughman came in with a woman who was under arrest for the murder of Two Shoes Running Bear. She was George's wife. While we documented the facts, she was locked in the holding cell. Three hours later, I found her hanging from the steam pipes above her cot. She used the sheets." Deputy Ted Paquin related the facts quickly.

"Call the undertaker to get the body. Damn, I hate this business. I'll be right there. Get that Victor, we're going to have a real interrogation right now." The sheriff shouted orders down the phone. "Make sure that bastard is in chains both feet and hands. We're getting to the bottom of things. I knew he was up to something. Wait 'til he hears she is dead."

A deputy was walking Victor into the sheriff's office in St. Ignace from the jail area as the stretcher passed with Isabel on it. He was chained at the ankles and cuffed behind at the wrists. He looked puzzled as he entered and stood in front of the desk looking at County Sheriff Brown.

"Sit down, Victor, do you know who that corpse is? It's Isabel, she hung herself. She heard about what you pulled. Do you want to tell me the rest of your story?"

Victor staggered, almost tripped from the tug of the leg irons, and fell slumped in a chair. He put his head on the table next to him without saying a word.

"So, she is dead, what are your plans now?"

Victor slowly raised his head and looked away, saying, "Why? Why did she do it? Because you told her I got caught with the money? It's your fault. You shouldn't have told her. Did she tell you how it happened?"

"That's why you're here. After getting the facts from her, many things conflicted, and some gave way to a solution to all this affair. Now it's your turn," County Sheriff Brown said. "You asked if she told how it happened. Yah, she sure did. She said she did it all, robbed Peabody, killed Two Shoes, and gave you the money to run away with. She said you promised her to take her down below. You, schmuck, you tried to ditch her, have all the money for yourself, and leave her hanging out to dry."

"Don't say that. Dammit, she lied. She told me about the money in the safe. We talked, she asked me what I thought about robbing the safe so we could escape this area. I agreed and took her tire iron to break in. She was big and tall, as you could see, but not strong enough to break in the door and safe. I did it. I gave her the onyx figurine. She worried that Two Shoes would see it, so I planned to kill him as soon as I could find him, the little Indian never sat in the same trail very long. Finally, she called me and told me she saw him head in the direction of the channel to fish. I waited until later in the evening so it wouldn't be very light out. I did it. I hit him and dragged him into his fishing spot. He said something just as he slid into the water that has haunted me ever since."

"What was that, Victor?"

"I could hardly hear him, but he said, 'Why.'"

Mackinaw County Sheriff Brown looked at Victor with disgust and said, "Lock him up for me, Ted." He looked at his watch and said, "It's three in the morning, I'll see you at nine. Good night."

CHAPTER TWENTY-NINE

A Secret Kept

George and Lightfoot rode silently out of town, north on the Dixie Highway. Lightfoot was giving George time to mull through the events leading up to Isabel's death.

"It's over," George said after twenty minutes had passed.

Lightfoot remained silent, letting George think and say what he needed to. They were headed east by this time.

"I regret we had to include Two Shoes' name as one of Isabel's lovers. I still have doubts about her story. But how else did she know about the money? Two Shoes was getting to the age where a man needs someone, a female someone, to confide in. I suppose it was innocent at first, but it led to a serious weight on his heart. How he must have suffered knowing he was in love with his friend's wife. He loved us both. If we eliminated the fact that he was her lover, she would have brought it up in court, so we had to. Strange how things go. Now she's dead, and it will never be said. Only the sheriff and deputies will know the details."

Lightfoot waited to see if he had more to say. However, George finally was tired and fell to sleep for the final few miles to the reservation where Lightfoot brought the Ford to a stop near his car. The full moon lighted the parking lot near the great hall. George woke when he felt the truck stop. He sat up and scratched his head, looked round, and could see where he was. Then it all came back in a rush. "Lightfoot, I have a confession to make to you. I hope you and the tribe don't hold it against me. Isabel told me I talk in my sleep. I have been afraid I may have told her indirectly too much."

"Excuse me, I didn't hear you," Lightfoot said. "You remember what you said just a few hours ago? It's over. You must look to the Great Spirit for his consoling, understanding, and looking to the future. Trust in his love."

George looked at him and believed he saw a slight smile on his face and a twinkle in his eyes.

The cold air woke him fully while he walked to his truck. He waved at his friend and said, "See you soon."

The short three miles to his home passed by quickly. He knew the fire would be out, so before he could get some sleep, he would need to build a fire. Then he would sleep until he was rested.

As his head hit the pillow, he already was talking to the creator of all things. Sleep came with a flowing assurance that all would be well.

CHAPTER THIRTY

What's the Scoop?

At nine the next morning, George received a call from the county sheriff with the news that Victor had confessed to everything and had vindicated Isabel. The weight was lifted from his shoulders, and he looked to the heavens in thanks. He smiled for the first time in several days.

Meanwhile, Lightfoot needed to pick up something from the hardware. He had a good rest and finally headed that way. He thought about what George was doing and headed to George's home first.

George answered the door in his long johns, his hair ruffled, and with sleep in his eyes. "Hi, Lightfoot, come on in." He stepped back and gestured a wide sweep for him to pass.

"How are you doing this morning, George?"

"Not bad considering. Have a cup of coffee." George pointed to the stove.

"Don't mind if I do." Lightfoot poured a mugful and sat down by the table where George sat. "Have you thought about what you will be faced with today and the following few days? I am here to help you through this, but please think about what you will have to do. It won't be easy to have to tell the countryside what took place in the last twenty-four hours."

"I have been thinking about it, and the best thing I can come up with is to have Maria interview me for the paper so I can tell my story. It's the only way they will understand everything, even if I don't tell everything. I've thought so much, and the way Maria puts it in the paper will be sufficient for me. I know she will write the words conceivably correct."

"In other words, George, you will make a broad explanation and pray everyone will understand?"

"That's right, Lightfoot. I thought I knew my wife. We were married ten years. She worked every day and never took a day off. She cooked and kept things together here, even when the washing would freeze as fast as she hung them up on the clothesline outdoors. Her hands ached from the cold, but she never complained. Oh, true, when she was tired, she was short with me. Just the same, she got over it, and everything was back to normal. How does a man tell the world what truly was on her heart and what she really was thinking?" George paused, and then he continued in a slower pace, "She didn't have a child. I don't know why, but I'm sure that was a disappointment to her as well as it was for me. I loved her differently than my first wife, but she was different. She said she was disappointed with the whole situation—the tiny home, the long winters, the slow pace in a remote area. Isabel just wanted to get away, and now she has."

George pushed away from the oak table and said, "Let's go over to the office. I'll talk to Maria, and maybe you can add anything I may leave out. What do you think, Lightfoot?"

"I'll tag along, but only until we finish the article because I have some duties at the reservation, and I need to check the trapline. And one more thing, isn't it time you called me something besides my last name?"

"Thanks and yes. What do you want me to call you? Robert or Bob?"

"Rob, that's what my friends call me," Lightfoot said.

"Okay, Rob, let's head over to the office as soon as I get dressed."

"Yah, for a minute, I thought you might have forgotten you are in your long johns only." Lightfoot grinned.

Maria was working in the news office when they entered the foyer. George went in followed by Lightfoot. She looked up from her work and smiled at the two. "Good morning, what's happening?"

George began to tell her what had happened the day before when the telephone rang in his office. He jumped up and answered it to find it was from the Mackinaw County Sheriff Office.

"George, after we talked last night, we interrogated Victor. He said Isabel lied for him. The fact is he was the true killer. He admitted everything. You can come in to read the complete report when you are ready."

"What makes you believe he is telling you the truth, Sheriff?"

"He knew exactly what Two Shoes said, his very last word."

George's heart jumped; he remembered Isabel hadn't mentioned anything about what Two Shoes had said. "And what was that, Sheriff?"

"Victor said he said in just over a whisper, 'Why?'"

"That's enough for me. Thanks for calling and giving this bit of information. It clarifies things and has a better closure to the case."

George came back in to the news office to add to what he was previously saying. "As I was saying, I wish to tell what happened, but if you would leave out some of the fine details."

She looked at him, confused.

"What I'm trying to say is, in order to notify the people what happened and how the crime, robbery, and murder were solved, I would like you to put an article in the news with an accurate account of what happened."

"All right, you tell me what you want put in the paper, George, and I'll publish it."

"Well, Rob, or Lightfoot, and I discussed how much we need to tell without giving you all the details. However, this telephone call changed a few facts, so I'll start here." George cleared his throat and began. "After investigating the crime of robbery and murder, I found to my surprise and much regret that it was my wife, Isabel Kaughman, who killed Two Shoes and committed the robbery."

"What?" Maria asked in shock.

"Let me finish and then you can ask me questions." George gave her an apologetic smile.

"Isabel was going through a state of depression and thought she wanted to get away from the area. There were several reasons why she was unhappy. She was childless, lacked the communication she had in the city, and was disillusioned with the meager living we shared, so nothing could appease her. She told us she decided to rob her supervisor, Mr. Peabody. She heard he had a safe full of money. She stole an onyx bear from Peabody as well and put it on her trinket shelf. In her state of mind, she believed Two Shoes would know she did the robbery if he saw the onyx bear when he came to visit, so she decided to murder him. Without thinking, she involved many people, which led her to be caught. In a panic, it appeared she thought she had nothing to live for, or in her remorse, she committed suicide."

"However, she lied for her friend, Victor, who after interrogation finally confessed to everything. He admitted that she told him about it and that they planned the robbery and murder, but Victor did the dirty work."

Marie took notes as George told the sad tale. Rob Lightfoot asked something about her obituary. "Maybe you can add, 'You can read the obituary details in the obituary column of this paper.'"

"Yes," Maria said. "I'll make sure I have the notice with details in case anyone will want to attend her funeral."

"Thanks, Maria. If you have any questions, just let me know. I'm going back home. I need some rest and quiet." He looked at Lightfoot and said, "Thanks, Rob, for being there for me."

Later when Lightfoot left the hardware with the tool he needed, he ran into Jeffery Beacom.

"What happened, Lightfoot?" Jeffery Beacom asked, even though he suspected.

"George made an arrest. We have a man in custody. Case closed."

"No, I mean, Isabel, what happened with her?"

"Read the paper. It will be out in a couple days."

Lightfoot looked down and mumbled something and turned toward his car.

Jeffery heard one word, "Later." He made a face and walked in the opposite direction.

CHAPTER THIRTY-ONE

A Lady's Farewell

A small group of people were entering the church on Bay Street at the Union Church. The organ played softly, and low voices were heard. A group of ladies sat in the front row on the left, while Peabody sat on the right. Wendell Peabody, George Kaufman, Robert Lightfoot, Maria Sutherland, the crew from school as well as teachers, Jeffery Beacom, and some of the locals sat waiting for the funeral service of Tilde Peabody.

A well-dressed woman sat in the last pew on the left. She had a veiled hat that matched her black woolen suit, along with her high-heeled shoes. Her hair was shoulder-length and dark auburn red. She sat silently, not looking at anyone. She was beautiful with a remarkable figure. Most people looked at her curiously. Some wondered who she was, others guessed, while a few knew but kept silent and away from her.

It all happened so fast. Tilde was washing dishes after dinner when Peabody heard a thud on the kitchen floor. He rushed in from his office to find Tilde lying with her eyes closed, silent, and with the dish towel still in her hand. He felt her wrist. There was no pulse, and then her neck, it was certain she was gone.

He rang up the doctor, who had gone home for the day. Doctor DeJour came as soon as he could, but there wasn't anything he could do for her.

Peabody had mixed feelings. He felt sorry Tilde was gone yet happy that he was free to be with Alice.

The short drive to the cemetery, a few words spoken, and Peabody left to the house. Tilde was at peace at last, she filled her spot in life, and did what was expected of her. Many thought she was special, a very amiable woman, who said very little and kept the peace. She truly would be missed by those who spent time with her in this life. Peabody went alone to the grave site. They had no relatives or children. A luncheon was served at the church by the ladies' group, some were ones who played cards with her weekly. Afterwards, the men walked west from the church to Cedarville Bar to socialize.

Peabody had put in for his retirement, which would be at the end of the current school year.

Two cars parked at Peabody's home, Peabody's and the well-built auburn red-haired stranger's. There was no reason for them to hide their relationship any longer. A marriage was planned in the future on their cruise to Jamaica.

CHAPTER THIRTY-TWO

A Positive View

Three days later, a small group gathered at the Lutheran Church on the hill on M-129 just north of Cedarville. A hearse parked near the door. Organ music could be heard all the way to the main road through Cedarville. The fat organ player sat on the stool, her upper arms jiggling like jelly. The reverend silently thought he should have picked a slower hymn.

There was George, his parents and brother, Lightfoot, Chief and Rowena, Jeffery Beacom, Maria Sutherland, Norman Peabody and his lady friend, Wilbert and Gilbert Sheppard and their wives, and Victoria and her husband plus a few more, including the couple who ran the little restaurant around the corner.

Of course, Peabody would be there; he was Isabel's boss, and it was natural that Victoria would attend the memorial service. She was the only friend Isabel had. She sat on the opposite side of the church away from George's family. She suspected but acted unaware of the things that happened, even though she heard the gossip and knew her brother, Victor, was sitting in the county jail in St. Ignace, waiting trial and sentencing until proven guilty.

Jeffery Beacom sat in the back near the door. He didn't want to miss anything or anyone. The huge oak doors were pushed open wide as Pierre Bouchard entered noisily. If it wasn't for the burgundy carpet, his footsteps would vibrate through the tall spans of the arch-carved beams to the very peak of the church. He sat with a thud.

176

Shortly after, the service began. The old minister had very little to say about Isabel. She had visited the church from time to time, but had never joined. The circumstances were unusual and left him uncomfortable, so he talked about those who remained, how they should look to our heavenly Father for guidance. He also stretched his sermon in the direction to those who "needed God" in their lives and the circumstances they took when our Lord was ignored. He mentioned how this was the loss of the second wife for George and that George was a very strong-willed and brave man to survive all that was delivered him.

George sat straight and silently thanked his Heavenly Father for the strength he had given him through all the ordeals in his life knowing he would never have survived without him. Peace settled over him, and a smile of thanks engulfed him with that piece of encouragement.

George's mother wanted to touch George, assuring him she was there for him, but stopped before following through. The service ended just abruptly as it had started. The reverend walked to the back and shook hands with those who departed to the dining room or out the exit.

The food smelled pretty good. Most went to the back where it was being served in the huge dining room doubly used for Sunday school classes.

Victoria and her husband went ahead of the crowd and exited without saying anything to anyone before the reverend reached them to shake their hands.

After the noon luncheon, George thanked Pierre, whom he was surprised to see; Wendell and Alice, who smiled in gratitude; his family, Mom, Dad, and brother, Fredrick; the young cook, at which George gave his brother a knowing look; and all the others for coming.

"George." His mother had a loose grip on his arm. "Your dad and I are near if and when you need anything. We love..." Her voice choked.

George put his arms around his mother and hugged her for a very long time. Words could not make the warmth of the love flowing from mother to son at that moment any better.

Soon all had departed to their various destinations with the exception of Rob Lightfoot, Maria Southerland, and lastly but undeniably and expected by this time, Jeffery Beacom, who always needed to be a part of what's going on.

George stood with Lightfoot and Maria on the steps, watching the group leave. "Isabel is where she wanted. She did show remorse in her actions, and it is my hopes she is in a better place."

Jeffery, who stood off to the side a bit, popped up and said, "Things will be better now. Yep, bad times are over for you, George. Your first wife and son, Two Shoes, and Isabel. Three times and out." His hands rested on his tiny hips while he hopped off the church steps and was on his way.

Audrey J. Fick (A. Jay) was born on October 25, 1938 in Detroit, Michigan. She earned a bachelor's degree in Liberal Studies with a minor in Creative Writing and emphasis in Criminal Justice from Lake Superior State University. She was a fiction editor for the fifth edition of *Border Crossing*, an international literary journal. Her book review of Mark Jacobs' *Forty Wolves* was published in the September 2015 edition of *Peace Corps Magazine*. She currently lives in Hessel, Michigan, located in the eastern Upper Peninsula.

Printed in the USA
CPSIA information can be obtained
at www.ICGtesting.com
LVHW041300261023
762181LV00026BA/175